U0469902

SHAKESPEARE'S SONNETS

莎士比亚十四行诗

珍藏本

〔英〕莎士比亚 著
梁宗岱 译

人民文学出版社
PEOPLE'S LITERATURE PUBLISHING HOUSE

图书在版编目（CIP）数据

莎士比亚十四行诗 : 珍藏本 / (英) 莎士比亚著 ; 梁宗岱译 . -- 北京 : 人民文学出版社 , 2024 (2025.3 重印)
ISBN 978-7-02-018498-9

Ⅰ . ①莎… Ⅱ . ①莎… ②梁… Ⅲ . ①十四行诗 – 诗集 – 英国 – 中世纪 Ⅳ . ① I561.23

中国国家版本馆 CIP 数据核字 (2024) 第 003047 号

责任编辑　卜艳冰　何炜宏
装帧设计　李苗苗

出版发行　人民文学出版社
社　　址　北京市朝内大街 166 号
邮政编码　100705

印　　制　凸版艺彩 (东莞) 印刷有限公司
经　　销　全国新华书店等

字　　数　80 千字
开　　本　787 毫米 ×1092 毫米　1/32
印　　张　8.875
插　　页　5
版　　次　2024 年 2 月北京第 1 版
印　　次　2025 年 3 月第 3 次印刷

书　　号　978-7-02-018498-9
定　　价　108.00 元

《写作中的威廉·莎士比亚》

石版套色印刷画，1877年
胡安·兰达（Juan Landa）作
现藏西班牙巴塞罗那博物馆

《莎士比亚十四行诗》首版全书

伦敦，1609年
（原书第116首误印为“119”）
现藏伦敦英国国家图书馆

SHAKE-SPEARES

SONNETS.

Neuer before Imprinted.

AT LONDON
By *G. Eld* for *T. T.* and are
to be solde by *Iohn Wright*, dwelling
at Christ Church gate.
1609.

TO. THE. ONLIE. BEGETTER. OF.
THESE. INSVING. SONNETS.
M[r]. W. H. ALL. HAPPINESSE.
AND. THAT. ETERNITIE.
PROMISED.

BY.

OVR. EVER-LIVING. POET.

WISHETH.

THE. WELL-WISHING.
ADVENTVRER. IN.
SETTING.
FORTH.

T. T.

SHAKE-SPEARES, SONNETS.

FRom faireſt creatures we deſire increaſe,
That thereby beauties *Roſe* might neuer die,
But as the riper ſhould by time deceaſe,
His tender heire might beare his memory:
But thou contracted to thine owne bright eyes,
Feed'ſt thy lights flame with ſelfe ſubſtantiall fewell,
Making a famine where aboundance lies,
Thy ſelfe thy foe,to thy ſweet ſelfe too cruell:
Thou that art now the worlds freſh ornament,
And only herauld to the gaudy ſpring,
Within thine owne bud burieſt thy content,
And tender chorle makſt waſt in niggarding:
Pitty the world,or elſe this glutton be,
To eate the worlds due,by the graue and thee.

2

VVHen fortie Winters ſhall beſeige thy brow,
And digge deep trenches in thy beauties field,
Thy youthes proud liuery ſo gaz'd on now,
Wil be a totter'd weed of ſmal worth held:
Then being askt,where all thy beautie lies,
Where all the treaſure of thy luſty daies;
To ſay within thine owne deepe ſunken eyes,
Were an all-eating ſhame,and thriftleſſe praiſe.
How much more praiſe deſeru'd thy beauties vſe,
If thou couldſt anſwere this faire child of mine
Shall ſum my count,and make my old excuſe
Proouing his beautie by ſucceſſion thine.

This were to be new made when thou art ould,
And see thy blood warme when thou feel'st it could,

3

LOoke in thy glasse and tell the face thou vewest,
Now is the time that face should forme an other,
Whose fresh repaire if now thou not renewest,
Thou doo'st beguile the world, vnblesse some mother.
For where is she so faire whose vn-eard wombe
Disdaines the tillage of thy husbandry?
Or who is he so fond will be the tombe,
Of his selfe loue to stop posterity?
Thou art thy mothers glasse and she in thee
Calls backe the louely Aprill of her prime,
So thou through windowes of thine age shalt see,
Dispight of wrinkles this thy goulden time.
But if thou liue remembred not to be,
Die single and thine Image dies with thee.

4

VNthrifty louelinesse why dost thou spend,
Vpon thy selfe thy beauties legacy?
Natures bequest giues nothing but doth lend,
And being franck she lends to those are free:
Then beautious nigard why doost thou abuse,
The bountious largesse giuen thee to giue?
Profitles vserer why doost thou vse
So great a summe of summes yet can'st not liue?
For hauing traffike with thy selfe alone,
Thou of thy selfe thy sweet selfe dost deceaue,
Then how when nature calls thee to be gone,
What acceptable *Audit* can'st thou leaue?
Thy vnus'd beauty must be tomb'd with thee,
Which vsed liues th'executor to be.

5

THose howers that with gentle worke did frame,
The louely gaze where euery eye doth dwell
Will play the tirants to the very same,

And

And that vnfaire which fairely doth excell:
For neuer resting time leads Summer on,
To hidious winter and confounds him there,
Sap checkt with frost and lustie leau's quite gon,
Beauty ore-snow'd and barenes euery where,
Then were not summers distillation left
A liquid prisoner pent in walls of glasse,
Beauties effect with beauty were bereft,
Nor it nor noe remembrance what it was.
But flowers distil'd though they with winter meete,
Leese but their show, their substance still liues sweet.

6

THen let not winters wragged hand deface,
In thee thy summer ere thou be distil'd:
Make sweet some viall; treasure thou some place,
With beautits treasure ere it be selfe kil'd:
That vse is not forbidden vsery,
Which happies those that pay the willing lone;
That's for thy selfe to breed an other thee,
Or ten times happier be it ten for one,
Ten times thy selfe were happier then thou art,
If ten of thine ten times refigur'd thee,
Then what could death doe if thou should'st depart,
Leauing thee liuing in posterity?
Be not selfe-wild for thou art much too faire,
To be deaths conquest and make wormes thine heire.

7

LOe in the Orient when the gracious light,
Lifts vp his burning head, each vnder eye
Doth homage to his new appearing sight,
Seruing with lookes his sacred maiesty,
And hauing climb'd the steepe vp heauenly hill,
Resembling strong youth in his middle age,
Yet mortall lookes adore his beauty still,
Attending on his goulden pilgrimage:
But when from high-most pich with wery car,

Like feeble age he reeleth from the day,
The eyes(fore dutious)now conuerted are
From his low tract and looke an other way:
So thou,thy selfe out-going in thy noon:
Vnlok'd on diest vnlesse thou get a sonne.

8

MVsick to heare,why hear'st thou musick sadly,
Sweets with sweets warre not , ioy delights in ioy:
Why lou'st thou that which thou receaust not gladly,
Or else receau'st with pleasure thine annoy?
If the true concord of well tuned sounds,
By vnions married do offend thine eare,
They do but sweetly chide thee, who confounds
In singlenesse the parts that thou should'st beare:
Marke how one string sweet husband to an other,
Strike each in each by mutuall ordering;
Resembling sier,and child, and happy mother,
Who all in one,one pleasing note do sing:
Whose speechlesse song being many,seeming one,
Sings this to thee thou single wilt proue none.

9.

IS it for feare to wet a widdowes eye,
That thou consum'st thy selfe in single life?
Ah;if thou issulesse shalt hap to die,
The world will waile thee like a makelesse wife,
The world wilbe thy widdow and still weepe,
That thou no forme of thee hast left behind,
When euery priuat widdow well may keepe,
By childrens eyes,her husbands shape in minde:
Looke what an vnthrift in the world doth spend
Shifts but his place,for still the world inioyes it
But beauties waste, hath in the world an end,
And kept vnvsde the vser so destroyes it:
No loue toward others in that bosome sits
That on himselfe such murdrous shame commits.

10

FOr ſhame deny that thou bear'ſt loue to any
Who for thy ſelfe art ſo vnprouident
Graunt if thou wilt,thou art belou'd of many,
But that thou none lou'ſt is moſt euident:
For thou art ſo poſſeſt with murdrous hate,
That gainſt thy ſelfe thou ſtickſt not to conſpire,
Seeking that beautious roofe to ruinate
Which to repaire ſhould be thy chiefe deſire:
O change thy thought,that I may change my minde,
Shall hate be fairer log'd then gentle loue?
Be as thy preſence is gracious and kind,
Or to thy ſelfe at leaſt kind harted proue,
Make thee an other ſelfe for loue of me,
That beauty ſtill may liue in thine or thee.

11

AS faſt as thou ſhalt wane ſo faſt thou grow'ſt,
In one of thine,from that which thou departeſt,
And that freſh bloud which yongly thou beſtow'ſt,
Thou maiſt call thine,when thou from youth conuerteſt,
Herein liues wiſdome,beauty,and increaſe,
Without this follie,age,and could decay,
If all were minded ſo,the times ſhould ceaſe,
And threeſcoore yeare would make the world away:
Let thoſe whom nature hath not made for ſtore,
Harſh,featureleſſe,and rude, barrenly perriſh,
Looke whom ſhe beſt indow'd,ſhe gaue the more;
Which bountious guift thou ſhouldſt in bounty cherriſh,
She caru'd thee for her ſeale,and ment therby,
Thou ſhouldſt print more,not let that coppy die.

12

VV Hen I doe count the clock that tels the time,
And ſee the braue day ſunck in hidious night,
When I behold the violet paſt prime,
And ſable curls or ſiluer'd ore with white:
When lofty trees I ſee barren of leaues,
Which erſt from heat did canopie the herd

And Sommers greene all girded vp in sheaues
Borne on the beare with white and bristly beard:
Then of thy beauty do I question make
That thou among the wastes of time must goe,
Since sweets and beauties do them-selues forsake,
And die as fast as they see others grow,
And nothing gainst Times sieth can make defence
Saue breed to braue him, when he takes thee hence.

13

O That you were your selfe, but loue you are
No longer yours, then you your selfe here liue,
Against this cumming end you should prepare,
And your sweet semblance to some other giue.
So should that beauty which you hold in lease
Find no determination, then you were
You selfe again after your selfes decease,
When your sweet issue your sweet forme should beare.
Who lets so faire a house fall to decay,
Which husbandry in honour might vphold,
Against the stormy gusts of winters day
And barren rage of deaths eternall cold?
O none but vnthrifts, deare my loue you know,
You had a Father, let your Son say so.

14

NOt from the stars do I my iudgement plucke,
And yet me thinkes I haue Astronomy,
But not to tell of good, or euil lucke,
Of plagues, of dearths, or seasons quallity,
Nor can I fortune to breefe mynuits tell;
Pointing to each his thunder, raine and winde,
Or say with Princes if it shal go wel
By oft predict that I in heauen finde.
But from thine eies my knowledge I deriue,
And constant stars in them I read such art
As truth and beautie shal together thriue
If from thy selfe, to store thou wouldst conuert:

Or

SONNETS.

Or else of thee this I prognosticate,
Thy end is Truthes and Beauties doome and date.

15

WHen I consider euery thing that growes
Holds in perfection but a little moment.
That this huge stage presenteth nought but showes
Whereon the Stars in secret influence comment.
When I perceiue that men as plants increase,
Cheared and checkt euen by the selfe-same skie:
Vaunt in their youthfull sap, at height decrease,
And were their braue state out of memory.
Then the conceit of this inconstant stay,
Sets you most rich in youth before my sight,
Where wastfull time debateth with decay
To change your day of youth to sullied night,
And all in war with Time for loue of you
As he takes from you, I ingraft you new.

16

BVt wherefore do not you a mightier waie
Make warre vppon this bloudie tirant time?
And fortifie your selfe in your decay
With meanes more blessed then my barren rime?
Now stand you on the top of happie houres,
And many maiden gardens yet vnset,
With vertuous wish would beare your liuing flowers,
Much liker then your painted counterfeit:
So should the lines of life that life repaire
Which this (Times pensel or my pupill pen)
Neither in inward worth nor outward faire
Can make you liue your selfe in eies of men,
To giue away your selfe, keeps your selfe still,
And you must liue drawne by your owne sweet skill.

17

VVHo will beleeue my verse in time to come
If it were fild with your most high deserts?

Though yet heauen knowes it is but as a tombe
Which hides your life, and ſhewes not halfe your parts:
If I could write the beauty of your eyes,
And in freſh numbers number all your graces,
The age to come would ſay this Poet lies,
Such heauenly touches nere toucht earthly faces.
So ſhould my papers (yellowed with their age)
Be ſcorn'd,like old men of leſſe truth then tongue,
And your true rights be termd a Poets rage,
And ſtretched miter of an Antique ſong.
  But were ſome childe of yours aliue that time,
  You ſhould liue twiſe in it,and in my rime.

18.

SHall I compare thee to a Summers day?
Thou art more louely and more temperate:
Rough windes do ſhake the darling buds of Maie,
And Sommers leaſe hath all too ſhort a date:
Sometime too hot the eye of heauen ſhines,
And often is his gold complexion dimm'd,
And euery faire from faire ſome-time declines,
By chance,or natures chãging courſe vntrim'd:
But thy eternall Sommer ſhall not fade,
Nor looſe poſſeſſion of that faire thou ow'ſt,
Nor ſhall death brag thou wandr'ſt in his ſhade,
When in eternall lines to time thou grow'ſt,
  So long as men can breath or eyes can ſee,
  So long liues this,and this giues life to thee,

19

DEuouring time blunt thou the Lyons pawes,
And make the earth deuoure her owne ſweet brood,
Plucke the keene teeth from the fierce Tygers yawes,
And burne the long liu'd Phænix in her blood,
Make glad and ſorry ſeaſons as thou fleet'ſt,
And do what ere thou wilt ſwift-footed time
To the wide world and all her fading ſweets:
But I forbid thee one moſt hainous crime,

O carue not with thy howers my loues faire brow,
Nor draw noe lines there with thine antique pen,
Him in thy course vntainted doe allow,
For beauties patterne to succeding men.
  Yet doe thy worst ould Time dispight thy wrong,
  My loue shall in my verse euer liue young.

20

A Womans face with natures owne hand painted,
Haste thou the Master Mistris of my passion,
A womans gentle hart but not acquainted
With shifting change as is false womens fashion,
An eye more bright then theirs, lesse false in rowling:
Gilding the obiect where-vpon it gazeth,
A man in hew all *Hews* in his controwling,
Which steales mens eyes and womens soules amaseth,
And for a woman wert thou first created,
Till nature as she wrought thee fell a dotinge,
And by addition me of thee defeated,
By adding one thing to my purpose nothing.
  But since she prickt thee out for womens pleasure,
  Mine be thy loue and thy loues vse their treasure.

21

SO is it not with me as with that Muse,
Stird by a painted beauty to his verse,
Who heauen it selfe for ornament doth vse,
And euery faire with his faire doth reherse,
Making a coopelment of proud compare
With Sunne and Moone, with earth and seas rich gems:
With Aprills first borne flowers and all things rare,
That heauens ayre in this huge rondure hems,
O let me true in loue but truly write,
And then beleeue me, my loue is as faire,
As any mothers childe, though not so bright
As those gould candells fixt in heauens ayer:
  Let them say more that like of heare-say well,
  I will not prayse that purpose not to sell.

22

MY glasse shall not perswade me I am ould,
So long as youth and thou are of one date,
But when in thee times forrwes I behould,
Then look I death my daies should expiate.
For all that beauty that doth couer thee,
Is but the seemely rayment of my heart,
Which in thy brest doth liue,as thine in me,
How can I then be elder then thou art?
O therefore loue be of thy selfe so wary,
As I not for my selfe,but for thee will,
Bearing thy heart which I will keepe so chary
As tender nurse her babe from faring ill,
Presume not on thy heart when mine is slaine,
Thou gau'st me thine not to giue backe againe.

23

AS an vnperfect actor on the stage,
Who with his feare is put besides his part,
Or some fierce thing repleat with too much rage,
Whose strengths abondance weakens his owne heart;
So I for feare of trust,forget to say,
The perfect ceremony of loues right,
And in mine owne loues strength seeme to decay,
Ore-charg'd with burthen of mine owne loues might:
O let my books be then the eloquence,
And domb presagers of my speaking brest,
Who pleade for loue,and look for recompence,
More then that tonge that more hath more exprest.
O learne to read what silent loue hath writ,
To heare wit eies belongs to loues fine wiht.

24

MIne eye hath play'd the painter and hath steeld,
Thy beauties forme in table of my heart,
My body is the frame wherein ti's held,
And perspectiue it is best Painters art.
For through the Painter must you see his skill,

To

To finde where your true Image pictur'd lies,
Which in my bosomes shop is hanging stil,
That hath his windowes glazed with thine eyes:
Now see what good-turnes eyes for eies haue done,
Mine eyes haue drawne thy shape, and thine for me
Are windowes to my brest, where-through the Sun
Delights to peepe, to gaze therein on thee
  Yet eyes this cunning want to grace their art
  They draw but what they see, know not the hart.

25

LEt those who are in fauor with their stars,
Of publike honour and proud titles bost,
Whilst I whome fortune of such tryumph bars
Vnlookt for ioy in that I honour most;
Great Princes fauorites their faire leaues spread,
But as the Marygold at the suns eye,
And in them-selues their pride lies buried,
For at a frowne they in their glory die.
The painefull warrier famosed for worth,
After a thousand victories once foild,
Is from the booke of honour rased quite,
And all the rest forgot for which he toild:
  Then happy I that loue and am beloued
  Where I may not remoue, nor be remoued.

26

LOrd of my loue, to whome in vassalage
Thy merrit hath my dutie strongly knit;
To thee I send this written ambassage
To witnesse duty, not to shew my wit.
Duty so great, which wit so poore as mine
May make seeme bare, in wanting words to shew it;
But that I hope some good conceipt of thine
In thy soules thought (all naked) will bestow it:
Til whatsoeuer star that guides my mouing,
Points on me gratiously with faire aspect,
And puts apparrell on my tottered louing,

To ſhow me worthy of their ſweet reſpect,
Then may I dare to boaſt how I doe loue thee,
Til then,not ſhow my head where thou maiſt proue me

27

WEary with toyle,I haſt me to my bed,
The deare repoſe for lims with trauaill tired,
But then begins a iourny in my head
To worke my mind,when boddies work's expired.
For then my thoughts(from far where I abide)
Intend a zelous pilgrimage to thee;
And keepe my drooping eye-lids open wide,
Looking on darknes which the blind doe ſee.
Saue that my ſoules imaginary ſight
Preſents their ſhaddoe to my ſightles view,
Which like a iewell(hunge in gaſtly night)
Makes blacke night beautious,and her old face new.
Loe thus by day my lims,by night my mind,
For thee,and for my ſelfe,noe quiet finde,

28

HOw can I then returne in happy plight
That am debard the benifit of reſt?
When daies oppreſſion is not eazd by night,
But day by night and night by day opreſt.
And each(though enimes to ethers raigne)
Doe in conſent ſhake hands to torture me,
The one by toyle,the other to complaine
How far I toyle,ſtill farther off from thee.
I tell the Day to pleaſe him thou art bright,
And do'ſt him grace when clouds doe blot the heauen:
So flatter I the ſwart complexiond night,
When ſparkling ſtars twire not thou guil'ſt th' eauen.
But day doth daily draw my ſorrowes longer,(ſtronger
And night doth nightly make greefes length ſeeme

29

VVHen in diſgrace with Fortune and mens eyes,
I all alone beweepe my out-caſt ſtate,

And

And trouble deafe heauen with my bootlesse cries,
And looke vpon my selfe and curse my fate.
Wishing me like to one more rich in hope,
Featur'd like him, like him with friends possest,
Desiring this mans art, and that mans skope,
With what I most inioy contented least,
Yet in these thoughts my selfe almost despising,
Haplye I thinke on thee, and then my state,
(Like to the Larke at breake of daye arising)
From sullen earth sings himns at Heauens gate,
For thy sweet loue remembred such welth brings,
That then I skorne to change my state with Kings.

30

VVHen to the Sessions of sweet silent thought,
I sommon vp remembrance of things past,
I sigh the lacke of many a thing I sought,
And with old woes new waile my deare times waste:
Then can I drowne an eye (vn-vs'd to flow)
For precious friends hid in deaths dateles night,
And weepe a fresh loues long since canceld woe,
And mone th'expence of many a vannisht sight.
Then can I greeue at greeuances fore-gon,
And heauily from woe to woe tell ore
The sad account of fore-bemoned mone,
Which I new pay as if not payd before.
But if the while I thinke on thee (deare friend)
All losses are restord, and sorrowes end.

31

THy bosome is indeared with all hearts,
Which I by lacking haue supposed dead,
And there raignes Loue and all Loues louing parts,
And all those friends which I thought buried.
How many a holy and obsequious teare
Hath deare religious loue stolne from mine eye,
As interest of the dead, which now appeare,
But things remou'd that hidden in there lie.

Thou art the graue where buried loue doth liue,
Hung with the tropheis of my louers gon,
Who all their parts of me to thee did giue,
That due of many,now is thine alone.
  Their images I lou'd, I view in thee,
  And thou(all they)haſt all the all of me.

32

IF thou ſuruiue my well contented daie,
When that churle death my bones with duſt ſhall couer
And ſhalt by fortune once more re-ſuruay:
Theſe poore rude lines of thy deceaſed Louer:
Compare them with the bett'ring of the time,
And though they be out-ſtript by euery pen,
Reſerue them for my loue, not for their rime,
Exceeded by the hight of happier men.
Oh then voutſafe me but this louing thought,
Had my friends Muſe growne with this growing age,
A dearer birth then this his loue had brought
To march in ranckes of better equipage:
  But ſince he died and Poets better proue,
  Theirs for their ſtile ile read,his for his loue.

33

FVll many a glorious morning haue I ſeene,
Flatter the mountaine tops with ſoueraine eie,
Kiſſing with golden face the meddowes greene;
Guilding pale ſtreames with heauenly alcumy:
Anon permit the baſeſt cloudes to ride,
With ougly rack on his celeſtiall face,
And from the for-lorne world his viſage hide
Stealing vnſeene to weſt with this diſgrace:
Euen ſo my Sunne one early morne did ſhine,
With all triumphant ſplendor on my brow,
But out alack,he was but one houre mine,
The region cloude hath mask'd him from me now.
  Yet him for this,my loue no whit diſdaineth,
  Suns of the world may ſtaine,whẽ heauens ſun ſtainteh.

34

VVHy didst thou promise such a beautious day,
And make me trauaile forth without my cloake,
To let bace cloudes ore-take me in my way,
Hiding thy brau'ry in their rotten smoke.
Tis not enough that through the cloude thou breake,
To dry the raine on my storme-beaten face,
For no man well of such a salue can speake,
That heales the wound, and cures not the disgrace:
Nor can thy shame giue phisicke to my griefe,
Though thou repent , yet I haue still the losse,
Th' offenders sorrow lends but weake reliefe
To him that beares the strong offenses losse.
Ah but those teares are pearle which thy loue sheeds,
And they are ritch, and ransome all ill deeds.

35

NO more bee greeu'd at that which thou hast done,
Roses haue thornes, and siluer fountaines mud,
Cloudes and eclipses staine both Moone and Sunne,
And loathsome canker liues in sweetest bud.
All men make faults, and euen I in this,
Authorizing thy trespas with compare,
My selfe corrupting saluing thy amisse,
Excusing their sins more then their sins are:
For to thy sensuall fault I bring in sence,
Thy aduerse party is thy Aduocate,
And gainst my selfe a lawfull plea commence,
Such ciuill war is in my loue and hate,
That I an accessary needs must be,
To that sweet theefe which sourely robs from me,

36

LEt me confesse that we two must be twaine,
Although our vndeuided loues are one:
So shall those blots that do with me remaine,
Without thy helpe, by me be borne alone.
In our two loues there is but one respect,

Though

Though in our liues a seperable spight,
Which though it alter not loues sole effect,
Yet doth it steale sweet houres from loues delight,
I may not euer-more acknowledge thee,
Least my bewailed guilt should do thee shame,
Nor thou with publike kindnesse honour me,
Vnlesse thou take that honour from thy name:
But doe not so, I loue thee in such sort,
As thou being mine, mine is thy good report.

37

AS a decrepit father takes delight,
To see his actiue childe do deeds of youth,
So I, made lame by Fortunes dearest spight
Take all my comfort of thy worth and truth.
For whether beauty, birth, or wealth, or wit,
Or any of these all, or all, or more
Intitled in their parts, do crowned sit,
I make my loue ingrafted to this store:
So then I am not lame, poore, nor dispis'd,
Whilst that this shadow doth such substance giue,
That I in thy abundance am suffic'd,
And by a part of all thy glory liue:
Looke what is best, that best I wish in thee,
This wish I haue, then ten times happy me.

38

HOw can my Muse want subiect to inuent
While thou dost breath that poor'st into my verse,
Thine owne sweet argument, to excellent,
For euery vulgar paper to rehearse:
Oh giue thy selfe the thankes if ought in me,
Worthy perusal stand against thy sight,
For who's so dumbe that cannot write to thee,
When thou thy selfe dost giue inuention light?
Be thou the tenth Muse, ten times more in worth
Then those old nine which rimers inuocate,
And he that calls on thee, let him bring forth

Eternall

Eternal numbers to out-liue long date.
If my ſlight Muſe doe pleaſe theſe curious daies,
The paine be mine,but thine ſhal be the praiſe.

39

OH how thy worth with manners may I ſinge,
When thou art all the better part of me?
What can mine owne praiſe to mine owne ſelfe bring;
And what is't but mine owne when I praiſe thee,
Euen for this,let vs deuided liue,
And our deare loue looſe name of ſingle one,
That by this ſeperation I may giue:
That due to thee which thou deſeru'ſt alone:
Oh abſence what a torment wouldſt thou proue,
Were it not thy ſoure leiſure gaue ſweet leaue,
To entertaine the time with thoughts of loue,
VVhich time and thoughts ſo ſweetly doſt deceiue.
And that thou teacheſt how to make one twaine,
By praiſing him here who doth hence remaine.

40

TAke all my loues,my loue,yea take them all,
What haſt thou then more then thou hadſt before?
No loue,my loue,that thou maiſt true loue call,
All mine was thine,before thou hadſt this more:
Then if for my loue,thou my loue receiueſt,
I cannot blame thee,for my loue thou vſeſt,
But yet be blam'd,if thou this ſelfe deceaueſt
By wilfull taſte of what thy ſelfe refuſeſt.
I doe forgiue thy robb'rie gentle theefe
Although thou ſteale thee all my pouerty:
And yet loue knowes it is a greater griefe
To beare loues wrong,then hates knowne iniury.
Laſciuious grace in whom all il wel ſhowes,
Kill me with ſpights yet we muſt not be foes.

41

THoſe pretty wrongs that liberty commits,
When I am ſome-time abſent from thy heart,

Thy beautie,and thy yeares full well befits,
For still temptation followes where thou art.
Gentle thou art,and therefore to be wonne,
Beautious thou art,therefore to be assailed.
And when a woman woes,what womans sonne,
Will sourely leaue her till he haue preuailed.
Aye me,but yet thou mighst my seate forbeare,
And chide thy beauty, and thy straying youth,
Who lead thee in their ryot euen there
Where thou art forst to breake a two-fold truth:
Hers by thy beauty tempting her to thee,
Thine by thy beautie beeing false to me.

42

THat thou hast her it is not all my griefe,
And yet it may be said I lou'd her deerely,
That she hath thee is of my wayling cheefe,
A losse in loue that touches me more neerely.
Louing offendors thus I will excuse yee,
Thou doost loue her,because thou knowst I loue her,
And for my sake euen so doth she abuse me,
Suffring my friend for my sake to approoue her,
If I loose thee,my losse is my loues gaine,
And loosing her,my friend hath found that losse,
Both finde each other,and I loose both twaine,
And both for my sake lay on me this crosse,
But here's the ioy,my friend and I are one,
Sweete flattery,then she loues but me alone.

43

WHen most I winke then doe mine eyes best see,
For all the day they view things vnrespected,
But when I sleepe,in dreames they looke on thee,
And darkely bright,are bright in darke directed.
Then thou whose shaddow shaddowes doth make bright,
How would thy shadowes forme,forme happy show,
To the cleere day with thy much cleerer light,
When to vn-seeing eyes thy shade shines so?

How

How would (I say) mine eyes be blessed made,
By looking on thee in the liuing day?
When in dead night their faire imperfect shade,
Through heauy sleepe on sightlesse eyes doth stay?
All dayes are nights to see till I see thee,
And nights bright daies when dreams do shew thee me,

44

IF the dull substance of my flesh were thought,
Iniurious distance should not stop my way,
For then dispight of space I would be brought,
From limits farre remote, where thou doost stay,
No matter then although my foote did stand
Vpon the farthest earth remoou'd from thee,
For nimble thought can iumpe both sea and land,
As soone as thinke the place where he would be.
But ah, thought kills me that I am not thought
To leape large lengths of miles when thou art gone,
But that so much of earth and water wrought,
I must attend, times leasure with my mone.
Receiuing naughts by elements so sloe,
But heauie teares, badges of eithers woe.

45

THe other two, slight ayre, and purging fire,
Are both with thee, where euer I abide,
The first my thought, the other my desire,
These present absent with swift motion slide.
For when these quicker Elements are gone
In tender Embassie of loue to thee,
My life being made of foure, with two alone,
Sinkes downe to death, opprest with melancholie.
Vntill liues composition be recured,
By those swift messengers return'd from thee,
Who euen but now come back againe assured,
Of their faire health, recounting it to me.
This told, I ioy, but then no longer glad,
I send them back againe and straight grow sad.

46

MIne eye and heart are at a mortall warre,
How to deuide the conquest of thy sight,
Mine eye, my heart their picture's sight would barre,
My heart, mine eye the freedome of that right,
My heart doth plead that thou in him doost lye,
(A closet neuer pearst with christall eyes)
But the defendant doth that plea deny,
And sayes in him their faire appearance lyes.
To side this title is impannelled
A quest of thoughts, all tennants to the heart,
And by their verdict is determined
The cleere eyes moyitie, and the deare hearts part.
As thus, mine eyes due is their outward part,
And my hearts right, their inward loue of heart.

47

BEtwixt mine eye and heart a league is tooke,
And each doth good turnes now vnto the other,
When that mine eye is famisht for a looke,
Or heart in loue with sighes himselfe doth smother;
With my loues picture then my eye doth feast,
And to the painted banquet bids my heart:
An other time mine eye is my hearts guest,
And in his thoughts of loue doth share a part.
So either by thy picture or my loue,
Thy seife away, are present still with me,
For thou nor farther then my thoughts canst moue,
And I am still with them, and they with thee.
Or if they sleepe, thy picture in my sight
Awakes my heart, to hearts and eyes delight.

48

HOw carefull was I when I tooke my way,
Each trifle vnder truest barres to thrust,
That to my vse it might vn-vsed stay
From hands of falsehood, in sure wards of trust?
But thou, to whom my iewels trifles are,

Most

Most worthy comfort,now my greatest griefe,
Thou best of deerest,and mine onely care,
Art left the prey of euery vulgar theefe.
Thee haue I not lockt vp in any chest,
Saue where thou art not,though I feele thou art,
Within the gentle closure of my brest,
From whence at pleasure thou maist come and part,
And euen thence thou wilt be stolne I feare,
For truth prooues theeuish for a prize so deare.

49

AGainst that time (if euer that time come)
When I shall see thee frowne on my defects,
When as thy loue hath cast his vtmost summe,
Cauld to that audite by aduis'd respects,
Against that time when thou shalt strangely passe,
And scarcely greete me with that sunne thine eye,
When loue conuerted from the thing it was
Shall reasons finde of setled grauitie.
Against that time do I insconce me here
Within the knowledge of mine owne desart,
And this my hand,against my selfe vpreare,
To guard the lawfull reasons on thy part,
To leaue poore me,thou hast the strength of lawes,
Since why to loue,I can alledge no cause.

50

HOw heauie doe I iourney on the way,
When what I seeke (my wearie trauels end)
Doth teach that ease and that repose to say
Thus farre the miles are measurde from thy friend.
The beast that beares me,tired with my woe,
Plods duly on,to beare that waight in me,
As if by some instinct the wretch did know
His rider lou'd not speed being made from thee:
The bloody spurre cannot prouoke him on,
That some-times anger thrusts into his hide,
Which heauily he answers with a grone,

More ſharpe to me then ſpurring to his ſide,
For that ſame grone doth put this in my mind,
My greefe lies onward and my ioy behind.

51

THus can my loue excuſe the ſlow offence,
Of my dull bearer, when from thee I ſpeed,
From where thou art, why ſhoulld I haſt me thence,
Till I returne of poſting is noe need.
O what excuſe will my poore beaſt then find,
When ſwift extremity can ſeeme but ſlow,
Then ſhould I ſpurre though mounted on the wind,
In winged ſpeed no motion ſhall I know,
Then can no horſe with my deſire keepe pace,
Therefore deſire (of perfects loue being made)
Shall naigh noe dull fleſh in his fiery race,
But loue, for loue, thus ſhall excuſe my iade,
Since from thee going, he went wilfull ſlow,
Towards thee ile run, and giue him leaue to goe.

52

SO am I as the rich whoſe bleſſed key,
Can bring him to his ſweet vp-locked treaſure,
The which he will not eu'ry hower ſuruay,
For blunting the fine point of ſeldome pleaſure.
Therefore are feaſts ſo ſollemne and ſo rare,
Since ſildom comming in the long yeare ſet,
Like ſtones of worth they thinly placed are,
Or captaine Iewells in the carconet.
So is the time that keepes you as my cheſt,
Or as the ward-robe which the robe doth hide,
To make ſome ſpeciall inſtant ſpeciall bleſt,
By new vnfoulding his impriſon'd pride.
Bleſſed are you whoſe worthineſſe giues skope,
Being had to tryumph, being lackt to hope.

53

VVHat is your ſubſtance, whereof are you made,
That millions of ſtrange ſhaddowes on you tend?

Since euery one,hath euery one,one ſhade,
And you but one,can euery ſhaddow lend:
Deſcribe *Adonis* and the counterfet,
Is poorely immitated after you,
On *Hellens* cheeke all art of beautie ſet,
And you in *Grecian* tires are painted new:
Speake of the ſpring,and foyzon of the yeare,
The one doth ſhaddow of your beautie ſhow,
The other as your bountie doth appeare,
And you in euery bleſſed ſhape we know.
 In all externall grace you haue ſome part,
 But you like none,none you for conſtant heart.

54

OH how much more doth beautie beautious ſeeme,
By that ſweet ornament which truth doth giue,
The Roſe lookes faire, but fairer we it deeme
For that ſweet odor,which doth in it liue:
The Canker bloomes haue full as deepe a die,
As the perfumed tincture of the Roſes,
Hang on ſuch thornes,and play as wantonly,
When ſommers breath their masked buds diſcloſes:
But for their virtue only is their ſhow,
They liue vnwoo'd, and vnreſpected fade,
Die to themſelues. Sweet Roſes doe not ſo,
Of their ſweet deathes, are ſweeteſt odors made:
 And ſo of you,beautious and louely youth,
 When that ſhall vade,by verſe diſtils your truth.

55

NOt marble, nor the guilded monument,
Of Princes ſhall out-liue this powrefull rime,
But you ſhall ſhine more bright in theſe contents
Then vnſwept ſtone, beſmeer'd with ſluttiſh time.
When waſtefull warre ſhall *Statues* ouer-turne,
And broiles roote out the worke of maſonry,
Nor *Mars* his ſword, nor warres quick fire ſhall burne:
The liuing record of your memory.

Gainst death, and all obliuious emnity
Shall you pace forth, your praise shall stil finde roome,
Euen in the eyes of all posterity
That weare this world out to the ending doome.
So til the iudgement that your selfe arise,
You liue in this, and dwell in louers eies.

56

Sweet loue renew thy force, be it not said
Thy edge should blunter be then apetite,
Which but too daie by feeding is alaied,
To morrow sharpned in his former might.
So loue be thou, although too daie thou fill
Thy hungrie eies, euen till they winck with fulnesse,
Too morrow see againe, and doe not kill
The spirit of Loue, with a perpetual dulnesse:
Let this sad *Intrim* like the Ocean be
Which parts the shore, where two contracted new,
Come daily to the banckes, that when they see:
Returne of loue, more blest may be the view.
As cal it Winter, which being ful of care,
Makes Sōmers welcome, thrice more wish'd, more rare:

57

BEing your slaue what should I doe but tend,
Vpon the houres, and times of your desire?
I haue no precious time at al to spend;
Nor seruices to doe til you require.
Nor dare I chide the world without end houre,
Whilst I (my soueraine) watch the clock for you,
Nor thinke the bitternesse of absence sowre,
VVhen you haue bid your seruant once adieue,
Nor dare I question with my iealious thought,
VVhere you may be, or your affaires suppose,
But like a sad slaue stay and thinke of nought
Saue where you are, how happy you make those.
So true a foole is loue, that in your Will,
(Though you doe any thing) he thinkes no ill.

58

THat God forbid, that made me first your slaue,
I should in thought controule your times of pleasure,
Or at your hand th' account of houres to craue,
Being your vassail bound to staie your leisure.
Oh let me suffer (being at your beck)
Th' imprison'd absence of your libertie,
And patience tame, to sufferance bide each check,
Without accusing you of iniury.
Be where you list, your charter is so strong,
That you your selfe may priuiledge your time
To what you will, to you it doth belong,
Your selfe to pardon of selfe-doing crime.
  I am to waite, though waiting so be hell,
  Not blame your pleasure be it ill or well.

59

IF their bee nothing new, but that which is,
Hath beene before, how are our braines beguild,
Which laboring for inuention beare amisse
The second burthen of a former child ?
Oh that record could with a back-ward looke,
Euen of fiue hundreth courses of the Sunne,
Show me your image in some antique booke,
Since minde at first in carrecter was done.
That I might see what the old world could say,
To this composed wonder of your frame,
Whether we are mended, or where better they,
Or whether reuolution be the same.
  Oh sure I am the wits of former daies,
  To subiects worse haue giuen admiring praise.

60

LIke as the waues make towards the pibled shore,
So do our minuites hasten to their end,
Each changing place with that which goes before,
In sequent toile all forwards do contend.
Natiuity once in the maine of light,

Crawles to maturity, wherewith being crown'd,
Crooked eclipses gainst his glory fight,
And time that gaue, doth now his gift confound.
Time doth transfixe the florish set on youth,
And delues the paralels in beauties brow,
Feedes on the rarities of natures truth,
And nothing stands but for his sieth to mow.
And yet to times in hope, my verse shall stand
Praising thy worth, dispight his cruell hand.

61

IS it thy wil, thy Image should keepe open
My heauy eielids to the weary night?
Dost thou desire my slumbers should be broken,
While shadowes like to thee do mocke my sight?
Is it thy spirit that thou send'st from thee
So farre from home into my deeds to prye,
To find out shames and idle houres in me,
The skope and tenure of thy Ielousie?
O no, thy loue though much, is not so great,
It is my loue that keepes mine eie awake,
Mine owne true loue that doth my rest defeat,
To plaie the watch-man euer for thy sake.
For thee watch I, whilst thou dost wake elsewhere,
From me farre of, with others all to neere.

62

SInne of selfe-loue possesseth al mine eie,
And all my soule, and al my euery part;
And for this sinne there is no remedie,
It is so grounded inward in my heart.
Me thinkes no face so gratious is as mine,
No shape so true, no truth of such account,
And for my selfe mine owne worth do define,
As I all other in all worths surmount.
But when my glasse shewes me my selfe indeed
Beated and chopt with tand antiquitie,
Mine owne selfe loue quite contrary I read

Selfe

Selfe, so selfe louing were iniquity,
T'is thee (my selfe) that for my selfe I praise,
Painting my age with beauty of thy daies,

63

AGainst my loue shall be as I am now
With times iniurious hand chrusht and ore-worne,
When houres haue dreind his blood and fild his brow
With lines and wrincles, when his youthfull morne
Hath trauaild on to Ages steepie night,
And all those beauties whereof now he's King
Are vanishing, or vanisht out of sight,
Stealing away the treasure of his Spring.
For such a time do I now fortifie
Against confounding Ages cruell knife,
That he shall neuer cut from memory
My sweet loues beauty, though my louers life.
His beautie shall in these blacke lines be seene,
And they shall liue, and he in them still greene.

64

VVHen I haue seene by times fell hand defaced
The rich proud cost of outworne buried age,
When sometime loftie towers I see downe rased,
And brasse eternall slaue to mortall rage.
When I haue seene the hungry Ocean gaine
Aduantage on the Kingdome of the shoare,
And the firme soile win of the watry maine,
Increasing store with losse, and losse with store.
When I haue seene such interchange of state,
Or state it selfe confounded, to decay,
Ruine hath taught me thus to ruminate
That Time will come and take my loue away.
This thought is as a death which cannot choose
But weepe to haue, that which it feares to loose.

65

SInce brasse, nor stone, nor earth, nor boundlesse sea,
But sad mortallity ore-swaies their power,

How with this rage shall beautie hold a plea,
Whose action is no stronger then a flower?
O how shall summers hunny breath hold out,
Against the wrackfull siedge of battring dayes,
When rocks impregnable are not so stoute,
Nor gates of steele so strong but time decayes?
O fearefull meditation, where alack,
Shall times best Iewell from times chest lie hid?
Or what strong hand can hold his swift foote back,
Or who his spoile or beautie can forbid?
  O none, vnlesse this miracle haue might,
  That in black inck my loue may still shine bright.

66

TYr'd with all these for restfull death I cry,
As to behold desert a begger borne,
And needie Nothing trimd in iollitie,
And purest faith vnhappily forsworne,
And gilded honor shamefully misplast,
And maiden vertue rudely strumpeted,
And right perfection wrongfully disgrac'd,
And strength by limping sway disabled,
And arte made tung-tide by authoritie,
And Folly (Doctor-like) controuling skill,
And simple-Truth miscalde Simplicitie,
And captiue-good attending Captaine ill.
  Tyr'd with all these, from these would I be gone,
  Saue that to dye, I leaue my loue alone.

67

AH wherefore with infection should he liue,
And with his presence grace impietie,
That sinne by him aduantage should atchiue,
And lace it selfe with his societie?
Why should false painting immitate his cheeke,
And steale dead seeing of his liuing hew?
Why should poore beautie indirectly seeke,
Roses of shaddow, since his Rose is true?

Why ſhould he liue,now nature banckrout is,
Beggerd of blood to bluſh through liuely vaines,
For ſhe hath no exchecker now but his,
And proud of many,liues vpon his gaines?
O him ſhe ſtores,to ſhow what welth ſhe had,
In daies long ſince,before theſe laſt ſo bad.

68

THus is his cheeke the map of daies out-worne,
When beauty liu'd and dy'ed as flowers do now,
Before theſe baſtard ſignes of faire were borne,
Or durſt inhabit on a liuing brow:
Before the goulden treſſes of the dead,
The right of ſepulchers,were ſhorne away,
To liue a ſcond life on ſecond head,
Ere beauties dead fleece made another gay:
In him thoſe holy antique howers are ſeene,
Without all ornament,it ſelfe and true,
Making no ſummer of an others greene,
Robbing no ould to dreſſe his beauty new,
And him as for a map doth Nature ſtore,
To ſhew faulſe Art what beauty was of yore.

69

THoſe parts of thee that the worlds eye doth view,
Want nothing that the thought of hearts can mend:
All toungs(the voice of ſoules)giue thee that end,
Vttring bare truth,euen ſo as foes Commend.
Their outward thus with outward praiſe is crownd,
But thoſe ſame toungs that giue thee ſo thine owne,
In other accents doe this praiſe confound
By ſeeing farther then the eye hath ſhowne.
They looke into the beauty of thy mind,
And that in gueſſe they meaſure by thy deeds,
Then churls their thoughts(although their eies were kind)
To thy faire flower ad the rancke ſmell of weeds,
But why thy odor matcheth not thy ſhow,
The ſolye is this,that thou doeſt common grow.

70

THat thou are blam'd shall not be thy defect,
For slanders marke was euer yet the faire,
The ornament of beauty is suspect,
A Crow that flies in heauens sweetest ayre.
So thou be good, slander doth but approue,
Their worth the greater beeing woo'd of time,
For Canker vice the sweetest buds doth loue,
And thou present'st a pure vnstayined prime.
Thou hast past by the ambush of young daies,
Either not assayld, or victor beeing charg'd,
Yet this thy praise cannot be soe thy praise,
To tye vp enuy, euermore inlarged,
If some suspect of ill maskt not thy show,
Then thou alone kingdomes of hearts shouldst owe.

71

NOe Longer mourne for me when I am dead,
Then you shall heare the surly sullen bell
Giue warning to the world that I am fled
From this vile world with vildest wormes to dwell:
Nay if you read this line, remember not,
The hand that writ it, for I loue you so,
That I in your sweet thoughts would be forgot,
If thinking on me then should make you woe.
O if (I say) you looke vpon this verse,
When I (perhaps) compounded am with clay,
Do not so much as my poore name reherse;
But let your loue euen with my life decay.
Least the wise world should looke into your mone,
And mocke you with me after I am gon.

72

O Least the world should taske you to recite,
What merit liu'd in me that you should loue
After my death (deare loue) for get me quite,
For you in me can nothing worthy proue.
Vnlesse you would deuise some vertuous lye,

To

To doe more for me then mine owne deſert,
And hang more praiſe vpon deceaſed I,
Then nigard truth would willingly impart:
O leaſt your true loue may ſeeme falce in this,
That you for loue ſpeake well of me vntrue,
My name be buried where my body is,
And liue no more to ſhame nor me,nor you.
For I am ſhamd by that which I bring forth,
And ſo ſhould you,to loue things nothing worth.

73

THat time of yeeare thou maiſt in me behold,
When yellow leaues,or none,or few doe hange
Vpon thoſe boughes which ſhake againſt the could,
Bare rn'wd quiers,where late the ſweet birds ſang.
In me thou ſeeſt the twi-light of ſuch day,
As after Sun-ſet fadeth in the Weſt,
Which by and by blacke night doth take away,
Deaths ſecond ſelfe that ſeals vp all in reſt.
In me thou ſeeſt the glowing of ſuch fire,
That on the aſhes of his youth doth lye,
As the death bed,whereon it muſt expire,
Conſum'd with that which it was nurriſht by.
This thou perceu'ſt,which makes thy loue more ſtrong,
To loue that well,which thou muſt leaue ere long.

74

BVt be contented when that fell areſt,
With out all bayle ſhall carry me away,
My life hath in this line ſome intereſt,
Which for memoriall ſtill with thee ſhall ſtay.
When thou reueweſt this,thou doeſt reuew,
The very part was conſecrate to thee,
The earth can haue but earth,which is his due,
My ſpirit is thine the better part of me,
So then thou haſt but loſt the dregs of life,
The pray of wormes,my body being dead,
The coward conqueſt of a wretches knife,

To

To base of thee to be remembred,
The worth of that, is that which it containes,
And that is this, and this with thee remaines.

75

SO are you to my thoughts as food to life,
Or as sweet season'd shewers are to the ground;
And for the peace of you I hold such strife,
As twixt a miser and his wealth is found.
Now proud as an inioyer, and anon
Doubting the filching age will steale his treasure,
Now counting best to be with you alone,
Then betterd that the world may see my pleasure,
Some-time all ful with feasting on your sight,
And by and by cleane starued for a looke,
Possessing or pursuing no delight
Saue what is had, or must from you be tooke.
Thus do I pine and surfet day by day,
Or gluttoning on all, or all away,

76

VVHy is my verse so barren of new pride?
So far from variation or quicke change?
Why with the time do I not glance aside
To new found methods, and to compounds strange?
Why write I still all one, euer the same,
And keepe inuention in a noted weed,
That euery word doth almost fel my name,
Shewing their birth, and where they did proceed?
O know sweet loue I alwaies write of you,
And you and loue are still my argument:
So all my best is dressing old words new,
Spending againe what is already spent:
For as the Sun is daily new and old,
So is my loue still telling what is told,

77

THy glasse will shew thee how thy beauties were,
Thy dyall how thy pretious mynuits waste,

The

The vacant leaues thy mindes imprint will beare,
And of this booke,this learning maist thou taste.
The wrinckles which thy glasse will truly show,
Of mouthed graues will giue thee memorie,
Thou by thy dyals shady stealth maist know,
Times theeuish progresse to eternitie.
Looke what thy memorie cannot containe,
Commit to these waste blacks,and thou shalt finde
Those children nurst,deliuerd from thy braine,
To take a new acquaintance of thy minde.
These offices,so oft as thou wilt looke,
Shall profit thee,and much inrich thy booke.

78

SO oft haue I inuok'd thee for my Muse,
And found such faire assistance in my verse,
As euery *Alien* pen hath got my vse,
And vnder thee their poesie disperse.
Thine eyes, that taught the dumbe on high to sing,
And heauie ignorance aloft to flie,
Haue added fethers to the learneds wing,
And giuen grace a double Maiestie.
Yet be most proud of that which I compile,
Whose influence is thine,and borne of thee,
In others workes thou doost but mend the stile,
And Arts with thy sweete graces graced be.
But thou art al my art,and doost aduance
As high as learning,my rude ignorance.

79

WHilst I alone did call vpon thy ayde,
My verse alone had all thy gentle grace,
But now my gracious numbers are decayde,
And my sick Muse doth giue an other place.
I grant (sweet loue)thy louely argument
Deserues the trauaile of a worthier pen,
Yet what of thee thy Poet doth inuent,
He robs thee of,and payes it thee againe,

He lends thee vertue, and he ſtole that word,
From thy behauiour, beautie doth he giue
And found it in thy cheeke: he can affoord
No praiſe to thee, but what in thee doth liue.
Then thanke him not for that which he doth ſay,
Since what he owes thee, thou thy ſelfe dooſt pay,

80

O How I faint when I of you do write,
Knowing a better ſpirit doth vſe your name,
And in the praiſe thereof ſpends all his might,
To make me toung-tide ſpeaking of your fame.
But ſince your worth (wide as the Ocean is)
The humble as the proudeſt ſaile doth beare,
My ſawſie barke (inferior farre to his)
On your broad maine doth wilfully appeare.
Your ſhalloweſt helpe will hold me vp a floate,
Whilſt he vpon your ſoundleſſe deepe doth ride,
Or (being wrackt) I am a worthleſſe bote,
He of tall building, and of goodly pride.
Then If he thriue and I be caſt away,
The worſt was this, my loue was my decay.

81

OR I ſhall liue your Epitaph to make,
Or you ſuruiue when I in earth am rotten,
From hence your memory death cannot take,
Although in me each part will be forgotten.
Your name from hence immortall life ſhall haue,
Though I (once gone) to all the world muſt dye,
The earth can yeeld me but a common graue,
When you intombed in mens eyes ſhall lye,
Your monument ſhall be my gentle verſe,
Which eyes not yet created ſhall ore-read,
And toungs to be, your beeing ſhall rehearſe,
When all the breathers of this world are dead,
You ſtill ſhall liue (ſuch vertue hath my Pen)
Where breath moſt breaths, euen in the mouths of men.

82

I Grant thou wert not married to my Muse,
And therefore maiest without attaint ore-looke
The dedicated words which writers vse
Of their faire subiect, blessing euery booke.
Thou art as faire in knowledge as in hew,
Finding thy worth a limmit past my praise,
And therefore art inforc'd to seeke anew,
Some fresher stampe of the time bettering dayes.
And do so loue, yet when they haue deuisde,
What strained touches Rhethorick can lend,
Thou truly faire, wert truly simpathizde,
In true plaine words, by thy true telling friend.
And their grosse painting might be better vs'd,
Where cheekes need blood, in thee it is abus'd.

83

I Neuer saw that you did painting need,
And therefore to your faire no painting set,
I found (or thought I found) you did exceed,
The barren tender of a Poets debt:
And therefore haue I slept in your report,
That you your selfe being extant well might show,
How farre a moderne quill doth come to short,
Speaking of worth, what worth in you doth grow,
This silence for my sinne you did impute,
Which shall be most my glory being dombe,
For I impaire not beautie being mute,
When others would giue life, and bring a tombe.
There liues more life in one of your faire eyes,
Then both your Poets can in praise deuise.

84

WHo is it that sayes most, which can say more,
Then this rich praise, that you alone, are you,
In whose confine immured is the store,
Which should example where your equall grew,
Leane penurie within that Pen doth dwell,

That to his ſubiect lends not ſome ſmall glory,
But he that writes of you,if he can tell,
That you are you,ſo dignifies his ſtory.
Let him but coppy what in you is writ,
Not making worſe what nature made ſo cleere,
And ſuch a counter-part ſhall fame his wit,
Making his ſtile admired euery where.
You to your beautious bleſſings adde a curſe,
Being fond on praiſe,which makes your praiſes worſe.

85

MY toung-tide Muſe in manners holds her ſtill,
While comments of your praiſe richly compil'd,
Reſerue their Character with goulden quill,
And precious phraſe by all the Muſes fil'd.
I thinke good thoughts,whilſt other write good wordes,
And like vnlettered clarke ſtill crie Amen,
To euery Himne that able ſpirit affords,
In poliſht forme of well refined pen.
Hearing you praiſd,I ſay 'tis ſo, 'tis true,
And to the moſt of praiſe adde ſome-thing more,
But that is in my thought,whoſe loue to you
(Though words come hind-moſt)holds his ranke before,
Then others,for the breath of words reſpect,
Me for my dombe thoughts,ſpeaking in effect.

86

VVAs it the proud full ſaile of his great verſe,
Bound for the prize of (all to precious) you,
That did my ripe thoughts in my braine inhearce,
Making their tombe the wombe wherein they grew?
Was it his ſpirit,by ſpirits taught to write,
Aboue a mortall pitch,that ſtruck me dead?
No,neither he,nor his compiers by night
Giuing him ayde,my verſe aſtoniſhed.
He nor that affable familiar ghoſt
Which nightly gulls him with intelligence,
As victors of my ſilence cannot boaſt,

I was

I was not sick of any feare from thence.
  But when your countinance fild vp his line,
  Then lackt I matter, that infeebled mine.

87

FArewell thou art too deare for my possessing,
And like enough thou knowst thy estimate,
The Charter of thy worth giues thee releasing:
My bonds in thee are all determinate.
For how do I hold thee but by thy granting,
And for that ritches where is my deseruing?
The cause of this faire guift in me is wanting,
And so my pattent back againe is sweruing.
Thy selfe thou gau'st, thy owne worth then not knowing,
Or mee to whom thou gau'st it, else mistaking,
So thy great guift vpon misprision growing,
Comes home againe, on better iudgement making.
  Thus haue I had thee as a dreame doth flatter,
  In sleepe a King, but waking no such matter.

88

VVHen thou shalt be dispode to set me light,
And place my merrit in the eie of skorne,
Vpon thy side, against my selfe ile fight,
And proue thee virtuous, though thou art forsworne:
With mine owne weakenesse being best acquainted,
Vpon thy part I can set downe a story
Of faults conceald, wherein I am attainted:
That thou in loosing me, shalt win much glory:
And I by this wil be a gainer too,
For bending all my louing thoughts on thee,
The iniuries that to my selfe I doe,
Doing thee vantage, duble vantage me,
  Such is my loue, to thee I so belong,
  That for thy right, my selfe will beare all wrong.

89

SAy that thou didst forsake mee for some falt,
And I will comment vpon that offence,

Speake of my lameneſſe, and I ſtraight will halt:
Againſt thy reaſons making no defence.
Thou canſt not (loue) diſgrace me halfe ſo ill,
To ſet a forme vpon deſired change,
As ile my ſelfe diſgrace, knowing thy wil,
I will acquaintance ſtrangle and looke ſtrange:
Be abſent from thy walkes and in my tongue,
Thy ſweet beloued name no more ſhall dwell,
Leaſt I (too much prophane) ſhould do it wronge:
And haplie of our old acquaintance tell.
For thee, againſt my ſelfe ile vow debate,
For I muſt nere loue him whom thou doſt hate.

90

THen hate me when thou wilt, if euer, now,
Now while the world is bent my deeds to croſſe,
Ioyne with the ſpight of fortune, make me bow,
And doe not drop in for an after loſſe:
Ah doe not, when my heart hath ſcapte this ſorrow,
Come in the rereward of a conquerd woe,
Giue not a windy night a rainie morrow,
To linger out a purpoſd ouer-throw.
If thou wilt leaue me, do not leaue me laſt,
When other pettie griefes haue done their ſpight,
But in the onſet come, ſo ſtall I taſte
At firſt the very worſt of fortunes might.
And other ſtraines of woe, which now ſeeme woe,
Compar'd with loſſe of thee, will not ſeeme ſo.

91

SOme glory in their birth, ſome in their skill,
Some in their wealth, ſome in their bodies force,
Some in their garments though new-fangled ill:
Some in their Hawkes and Hounds, ſome in their Horſe.
And euery humor hath his adiunct pleaſure,
Wherein it findes a ioy aboue the reſt,
But theſe perticulers are not my meaſure,
All theſe I better in one generall beſt.

Thy

Thy loue is bitter then high birth to me,
Richer then wealth, prouder then garments cost,
Of more delight then Hawkes or Horses bee:
And hauing thee, of all mens pride I boast.
Wretched in this alone, that thou maist take,
All this away, and me most wretched make.

92

BVt doe thy worst to steale thy selfe away,
For tearme of life thou art assured mine,
And life no longer then thy loue will stay,
For it depends vpon that loue of thine.
Then need I not to feare the worst of wrongs,
When in the least of them my life hath end,
I see, a better state to me belongs
Then that, which on thy humor doth depend.
Thou canst not vex me with inconstant minde,
Since that my life on thy reuolt doth lie,
Oh what a happy title do I finde,
Happy to haue thy loue, happy to die!
But whats so blessed faire that feares no blot,
Thou maist be falce, and yet I know it not.

93

SO shall I liue, supposing thou art true,
Like a deceiued husband, so loues face,
May still seeme loue to me, though alter'd new:
Thy lookes with me, thy heart in other place.
For their can liue no hatred in thine eye,
Therefore in that I cannot know thy change,
In manies lookes, the falce hearts history
Is writ in moods and frounes and wrinckles strange.
But heauen in thy creation did decree,
That in thy face sweet loue should euer dwell,
What ere thy thoughts, or thy hearts workings be,
Thy lookes should nothing thence, but sweetnesse tell.
How like *Eaues* apple doth thy beauty grow,
If thy sweet vertue answere not thy show.

94

THey that haue powre to hurt, and will doe none,
That doe not do the thing, they most do showe,
Who mouing others, are themselues as stone,
Vnmooued, could, and to temptation slow:
They rightly do inherrit heauens graces,
And husband natures ritches from expence,
They are the Lords and owners of their faces,
Others, but stewards of their excellence:
The sommers flowre is to the sommer sweet,
Though to it selfe, it onely liue and die,
But if that flowre with base infection meete,
The basest weed out-braues his dignity:
For sweetest things turne sowrest by their deedes,
Lillies that fester, smell far worse then weeds.

95

HOw sweet and louely dost thou make the shame,
Which like a canker in the fragrant Rose,
Doth spot the beautie of thy budding name?
Oh in what sweets doest thou thy sinnes inclose!
That tongue that tells the story of thy daies,
(Making lasciuious comments on thy sport)
Cannot dispraise, but in a kinde of praise,
Naming thy name, blesses an ill report.
Oh what a mansion haue those vices got,
Which for their habitation chose out thee,
Where beauties vaile doth couer euery blot,
And all things turnes to faire, that eies can see!
Take heed (deare heart) of this large priuiledge,
The hardest knife ill vs'd doth loose his edge.

96

SOme say thy fault is youth, some wantonesse,
Some say thy grace is youth and gentle sport,
Both grace and faults are lou'd of more and lesse:
Thou makst faults graces, that to thee resort:
As on the finger of a throned Queene,

The basest Iewell wil be well esteem'd:
So are those errors that in thee are seene,
To truths translated, and for true things deem'd.
How many Lambs might the sterne Wolfe betray,
If like a Lambe he could his lookes translate.
How many gazers mighst thou lead away,
If thou wouldst vse the strength of all thy state?
But doe not so, I loue thee in such sort,
As thou being mine, mine is thy good report.

97

HOw like a Winter hath my absence beene
From thee, the pleasure of the fleeting yeare?
What freezings haue I felt, what darke daies seene?
What old Decembers barenesse euery where?
And yet this time remou'd was sommers time,
The teeming Autumne big with ritch increase,
Bearing the wanton burthen of the prime,
Like widdowed wombes after their Lords decease:
Yet this aboundant issue seem'd to me,
But hope of Orphans, and vn-fathered fruite,
For Sommer and his pleasures waite on thee,
And thou away, the very birds are mute.
Or if they sing, tis with so dull a cheere,
That leaues looke pale, dreading the Winters neere.

98

FRom you haue I beene absent in the spring,
When proud pide Aprill (drest in all his trim)
Hath put a spirit of youth in euery thing:
That heauie *Saturne* laught and leapt with him.
Yet nor the laies of birds, nor the sweet smell
Of different flowers in odor and in hew,
Could make me any summers story tell:
Or from their proud lap pluck them where they grew:
Nor did I wonder at the Lillies white,
Nor praise the deepe vermillion in the Rose,
They weare but sweet, but figures of delight:

Drawne after you, you patterne of all those.
  Yet seem'd it Winter still, and you away,
  As with your shaddow I with these did play.

99

THe forward violet thus did I chide,
Sweet theefe whence didst thou steale thy sweet that
If not from my loues breath, the purple pride, (smels
Which on thy soft cheeke for complexion dwells?
In my loues veines thou hast too grosely died,
The Lillie I condemned for thy hand,
And buds of marierom had stolne thy haire,
The Roses fearefully on thornes did stand,
Our blushing shame, an other white dispaire:
A third nor red, nor white, had stolne of both,
And to his robbry had annext thy breath,
But for his theft in pride of all his growth
A vengfull canker eate him vp to death.
  More flowers I noted, yet I none could see,
  But sweet, or culler it had stolne from thee.

100

VV Here art thou Muse that thou forgetst so long,
To speake of that which giues thee all thy might?
Spendst thou thy furie on some worthlesse songe,
Darkning thy powre to lend base subiects light.
Returne forgetfull Muse, and straight redeeme,
In gentle numbers time so idely spent,
Sing to the eare that doth thy laies esteeme,
And giues thy pen both skill and argument.
Rise resty Muse, my loues sweet face suruay,
If time haue any wrincle grauen there,
If any, be a *Satire* to decay,
And make times spoiles dispised euery where.
  Giue my loue fame faster then time wasts life,
  So thou preuenst his sieth, and crooked knife.

101

OH truant Muse what shalbe thy amends,

For

For thy neglect of truth in beauty di'd?
Both truth and beauty on my loue depends:
So dost thou too, and therein dignifi'd:
Make answere Muse, wilt thou not haply saie,
Truth needs no collour with his collour fixt,
Beautie no pensell, beauties truth to lay:
But best is best, if neuer intermixt.
Because he needs no praise, wilt thou be dumb?
Excuse not silence so, for't lies in thee,
To make him much out-liue a gilded tombe:
And to be praisd of ages yet to be.
  Then do thy office Muse, I teach thee how,
  To make him seeme long hence, as he showes now.

102

My loue is strengthned though more weake in see-
I loue not lesse, thogh lesse the show appeare, (ming
That loue is marchandiz'd, whose ritch esteeming,
The owners tongue doth publish euery where.
Our loue was new, and then but in the spring,
When I was wont to greet it with my laies,
As *Philomell* in summers front doth singe,
And stops his pipe in growth of riper daies:
Not that the summer is lesse pleasant now
Then when her mournefull himns did hush the night,
But that wild musick burthens euery bow,
And sweets growne common loose their deare delight.
  Therefore like her, I some-time hold my tongue:
  Because I would not dull you with my songe.

103

Alack what pouerty my Muse brings forth,
That hauing such a skope to show her pride,
The argument all bare is of more worth
Then when it hath my added praise beside.
Oh blame me not if I no more can write!
Looke in your glasse and there appeares a face,
That ouer-goes my blunt inuention quite,
Dulling my lines, and doing me disgrace.

Were it not sinfull then striuing to mend,
To marre the subiect that before was well,
For to no other passe my verses tend,
Then of your graces and your gifts to tell.
And more, much more then in my verse can sit,
Your owne glasse showes you, when you looke in it.

104

TO me faire friend you neuer can be old,
For as you were when first your eye I eyde,
Such seemes your beautie still: Three Winters colde,
Haue from the forrests shooke three summers pride,
Three beautious springs to yellow *Autumne* turn'd,
In processe of the seasons haue I seene,
Three Aprill perfumes in three hot Iunes burn'd,
Since first I saw you fresh which yet are greene.
Ah yet doth beauty like a Dyall hand,
Steale from his figure, and no pace perceiu'd,
So your sweete hew, which me thinkes still doth stan[d]
Hath motion, and mine eye may be deceaued.
For feare of which, heare this thou age vnbred,
Ere you were borne was beauties summer dead.

105

LEt not my loue be cal'd Idolatrie,
Nor my beloued as an Idoll show,
Since all alike my songs and praises be
To one, of one, still such, and euer so.
Kinde is my loue to day, to morrow kinde,
Still constant in a wondrous excellence,
Therefore my verse to constancie confin'de,
One thing expressing, leaues out difference.
Faire, kinde, and true, is all my argument,
Faire, kinde and true, varrying to other words,
And in this change is my inuention spent,
Three theams in one, which wondrous scope affords.
Faire, kinde, and true, haue often liu'd alone.
Which three till now, neuer kept seate in one.

When

106

WHen in the Chronicle of wasted time,
I see discriptions of the fairest wights,
And beautie making beautifull old rime,
In praise of Ladies dead,and louely Knights,
Then in the blazon of sweet beauties best,
Of hand,of foote,of lip,of eye,of brow,
I see their antique Pen would haue exprest,
Euen such a beauty as you maister now.
So all their praises are but prophesies
Of this our time,all you prefiguring,
And for they look'd but with deuining eyes,
They had not still enough your worth to sing:
For we which now behold these present dayes,
Haue eyes to wonder,but lack toungs to praise.

107

NOt mine owne feares,nor the prophetick soule,
Of the wide world,dreaming on things to come,
Can yet the lease of my true loue controule,
Supposde as forfeit to a confin'd doome.
The mortall Moone hath her eclipse indur'de,
And the sad Augurs mock their owne presage,
Incertenties now crowne them-selues assur'de,
And peace proclaimes Oliues of endlesse age,
Now with the drops of this most balmie time,
My loue lookes fresh,and death to me subscribes,
Since spight of him Ile liue in this poore rime,
While he insults ore dull and speachlesse tribes.
And thou in this shalt finde thy monument,
When tyrants crests and tombs of brasse are spent.

108

VVHat's in the braine that Inck may character,
Which hath not figur'd to thee my true spirit,
What's new to speake,what now to register,
That may expresse my loue,or thy deare merit?
Nothing sweet boy,but yet like prayers diuine,

I muſt each day ſay ore the very ſame,
Counting no old thing old, thou mine, I thine,
Euen as when firſt I hallowed thy faire name.
So that eternall loue in loues freſh caſe,
Waighes not the duſt and iniury of age,
Nor giues to neceſſary wrinckles place,
But makes antiquitie for aye his page,
  Finding the firſt conceit of loue there bred,
  Where time and outward forme would ſhew it dead,

109

O Neuer ſay that I was falſe of heart,
Though abſence ſeem'd my flame to quallifie,
As eaſie might I from my ſelfe depart,
As from my ſoule which in thy breſt doth lye:
That is my home of loue, if I haue rang'd,
Like him that trauels I returne againe,
Iuſt to the time, not with the time exchang'd,
So that my ſelfe bring water for my ſtaine,
Neuer beleeue though in my nature raign'd,
All frailties that beſiege all kindes of blood,
That it could ſo prepoſterouſlie be ſtain'd,
To leaue for nothing all thy ſumme of good:
  For nothing this wide Vniuerſe I call,
  Saue thou my Roſe, in it thou art my all.

110

ALas 'tis true, I haue gone here and there,
And made my ſelfe a motley to the view,
Gor'd mine own thoughts, ſold cheap what is moſt deare,
Made old offences of affections new.
Moſt true it is, that I haue lookt on truth
Aſconce and ſtrangely: But by all aboue,
Theſe blenches gaue my heart an other youth,
And worſe eſſaies prou'd thee my beſt of loue,
Now all is done, haue what ſhall haue no end,
Mine appetite I neuer more will grin'de
On newer proofe, to trie an older friend,
A God in loue, to whom I am confin'd.

Then

Then giue me welcome, next my heauen the beſt,
Euen to thy pure and moſt moſt louing breſt.

111

O For my ſake doe you wiſh fortune chide,
The guiltie goddeſſe of my harmfull deeds,
That did not better for my life prouide,
Then publick meanes which publick manners breeds.
Thence comes it that my name receiues a brand,
And almoſt thence my nature is ſubdu'd
To what it workes in, like the Dyers hand,
Pitty me then, and wiſh I were renu'de,
Whilſt like a willing pacient I will drinke,
Potions of Eyſell gainſt my ſtrong infection,
No bitterneſſe that I will bitter thinke,
Nor double pennance to correct correction.
Pittie me then deare friend, and I aſſure yee,
Euen that your pittie is enough to cure mee.

112

YOur loue and pittie doth th'impreſſion fill,
Which vulgar ſcandall ſtampt vpon my brow,
For what care I who calles me well or ill,
So you ore-greene my bad, my good alow?
You are my All the world, and I muſt ſtriue,
To know my ſhames and praiſes from your tounge,
None elſe to me, nor I to none aliue,
That my ſteel'd ſence or changes right or wrong,
In ſo profound *Abiſme* I throw all care
Of others voyces, that my Adders ſence,
To cryttick and to flatterer ſtopped are:
Marke how with my neglect I doe diſpence.
You are ſo ſtrongly in my purpoſe bred,
That all the world beſides me thinkes y'are dead.

113

SInce I left you, mine eye is in my minde,
And that which gouernes me to goe about,
Doth part his function, and is partly blind,

Seemes

Seemes seeing,but effectually is out:
For it no forme deliuers to the heart
Of bird,of flowre,or shape which it doth lack,
Of his quick obiects hath the minde no part,
Nor his owne vision houlds what it doth catch:
For if it see the rud'st or gentlest sight,
The most sweet-fauor or deformedst creature,
The mountaine,or the sea,the day,or night:
The Croe,or Doue,it shapes them to your feature.
  Incapable of more repleat,with you,
  My most true minde thus maketh mine vntrue.

114

OR whether doth my minde being crown'd with you
Drinke vp the monarks plague this flattery?
Or whether shall I say mine eie saith true,
And that your loue taught it this *Alcumie*?
To make of monsters,and things indigest,
Such cherubines as your sweet selfe resemble,
Creating euery bad a perfect best
As fast as obiects to his beames assemble:
Oh tis the first,tis flatry in my seeing,
And my great minde most kingly drinkes it vp,
Mine eie well knowes what with his gust is greeing,
And to his pallat doth prepare the cup.
  If it be poison'd,tis the lesser sinne,
  That mine eye loues it and doth first beginne.

115

THose lines that I before haue writ doe lie,
Euen those that said I could not loue you deerer,
Yet then my iudgement knew no reason why,
My most full flame should afterwards burne cleerer.
But reckening time,whose milliond accidents
Creepe in twixt vowes,and change decrees of Kings,
Tan sacred beautie,blunt the sharp'st intents,
Diuert strong mindes to th' course of altring things:
Alas why fearing of times tiranie,

Might

Might I not then ſay now I loue you beſt,
When I was certaine ore in-certainty,
Crowning the preſent,doubting of the reſt:
Loue is a Babe, then might I not ſay ſo
To giue full growth to that which ſtill doth grow.

119

LEt me not to the marriage of true mindes
Admit impediments,loue is not loue
Which alters when it alteration findes,
Or bends with the remouer to remoue.
O no,it is an euer fixed marke
That lookes on tempeſts and is neuer ſhaken;
It is the ſtar to euery wandring barke,
Whoſe worths vnknowne,although his higth be taken.
Lou's not Times foole,though roſie lips and cheeks
Within his bending ſickles compaſſe come,
Loue alters not with his breefe houres and weekes,
But beares it out euen to the edge of doome:
If this be error and vpon me proued,
I neuer writ,nor no man euer loued.

117

ACcuſe me thus,that I haue ſcanted all,
Wherein I ſhould your great deſerts repay,
Forgot vpon your deareſt loue to call,
Whereto al bonds do tie me day by day,
That I haue frequent binne with vnknown mindes,
And giuen to time your owne deare purchaſ'd right,
That I haue hoyſted ſaile to al the windes
Which ſhould tranſport me fartheſt from your ſight.
Booke both my wilfulneſſe and errors downe,
And on iuſt proofe ſurmiſe,accumilate,
Bring me within the leuel of your frowne,
But ſhoote not at me in your wakened hate:
Since my appeale ſaies I did ſtriue to prooue
The conſtancy and virtue of your loue

118

LIke as to make our appetites more keene
With eager compounds we our pallat vrge,
As to preuent our malladies vnſeene,
We ſicken to ſhun ſickneſſe when we purge.
Euen ſo being full of your nere cloying ſweetneſſe,
To bitter ſawces did I frame my feeding;
And ſicke of wel-fare found a kind of meetneſſe,
To be diſeaſ'd ere that there was true needing.
Thus pollicie in loue t'anticipate
The ills that were, not grew to faults aſſured,
And brought to medicine a healthfull ſtate
Which rancke of goodneſſe would by ill be cured.
But thence I learne and find the leſſon true,
Drugs poyſon him that ſo fell ſicke of you.

119

WHat potions haue I drunke of *Syren* teares
Diſtil'd from Lymbecks foule as hell within,
Applying feares to hopes, and hopes to feares,
Still looſing when I ſaw my ſelfe to win?
What wretched errors hath my heart committed,
Whilſt it hath thought it ſelfe ſo bleſſed neuer?
How haue mine eies out of their Spheares bene fitted
In the diſtraction of this madding feuer?
O benefit of ill, now I find true
That better is, by euil ſtill made better.
And ruin'd loue when it is built anew
Growes fairer then at firſt, more ſtrong, far greater.
So I returne rebukt to my content,
And gaine by ills thriſe more then I haue ſpent.

120

THat you were once vnkind be-friends mee now,
And for that ſorrow , which I then didde feele,
Needes muſt I vnder my tranſgreſſion bow,
Vnleſſe my Nerues were braſſe or hammered ſteele.
For if you were by my vnkindneſſe ſhaken

As I by yours , y'haue past a hell of Time,
And I a tyrant haue no leasure taken
To waigh how once I suffered in your crime.
O that our night of wo might haue remembred
My deepest sence,how hard true sorrow hits,
And soone to you,as you to me then tendred
The humble salue,which wounded bosomes fits!
But that your trespasse now becomes a fee,
Mine ransoms yours,and yours must ransome mee,

121

TIS better to be vile then vile esteemed,
When not to be,receiues reproach of being,
And the iust pleasure lost,which is so deemed,
Not by our feeling,but by others seeing.
For why should others false adulterat eyes
Giue salutation to my sportiue blood?
Or on my frailties why are frailer spies;
Which in their wils count bad what I think good?
Noe, I am that I am,and they that leuell
At my abuses,reckon vp their owne,
I may be straight though they them-selues be beuel
By their rancke thoughtes,my deedes must not be shown
Vnlesse this generall euill they maintaine,
All men are bad and in their badnesse raigne.

122.

THy guift,,thy tables,are within my braine
Full characterd with lasting memory,
Which shall aboue that idle rancke remaine
Beyond all date euen to eternity.
Or at the least,so long as braine and heart
Haue facultie by nature to subsist,
Til each to raz'd obliuion yeeld his part
Of thee,thy record neuer can be mist:
That poore retention could not so much hold,
Nor need I tallies thy deare loue to skore,
Therefore to giue them from me was I bold,

To truſt thoſe tables that receaue thee more,
  To keepe an adiunckt to remember thee,
  Were to import forgetfulneſſe in mee.

123

NO! Time, thou ſhalt not boſt that I doe change,
Thy pyramyds buylt vp with newer might
To me are nothing nouell,nothing ſtrange,
They are but dreſſings of a former ſight:
Our dates are breefe,and therefor we admire,
What thou doſt foyſt vpon vs that is ould,
And rather make them borne to our deſire,
Then thinke that we before haue heard them tould:
Thy regiſters and thee I both defie,
Not wondring at the preſent,nor the paſt,
For thy records,and what we ſee doth lye,
Made more or les by thy continuall haſt:
  This I doe vow and this ſhall euer be,
  I will be true diſpight thy ſyeth and thee.

124

YF my deare loue were but the childe of ſtate,
It might for fortunes baſterd be vnfathered,
As ſubiect to times loue,or to times hate,
Weeds among weeds,or flowers with flowers gatherd.
No it was buylded far from accident,
It ſuffers not in ſmilinge pomp,nor falls
Vnder the blow of thralled diſcontent,
Whereto th'inuiting time our faſhion calls:
It feares not policy that *Heriticke*,
Which workes on leaſes of ſhort numbred howers,
But all alone ſtands hugely pollitick,
That it nor growes with heat,nor drownes with ſhowres.
  To this I witnes call the foles of time,
  Which die for goodnes,who haue liu'd for crime.

125

VVEr't ought to me I bore the canopy,
With my extern the outward honoring,

Or

Or layd great bases for eternity,
Which proues more short then wast or ruining?
Haue I not seene dwellers on forme and fauor
Lose all,and more by paying too much rent
For compound sweet;Forgoing simple sauor,
Pittifull thriuors in their gazing spent.
Noe,let me be obsequious in thy heart,
And take thou my oblacion,poore but free,
Which is not mixt with seconds,knows no art,
But mutuall render.onely me for thee.
  Hence,thou subbornd *Informer*, a trew soule
  When most impeacht,stands least in thy controule.

126

O Thou my louely Boy who in thy power,
Doest hould times fickle glasse,his sickle,hower:
Who hast by wayning growne,and therein shou'st,
Thy louers withering,as thy sweet selfe grow'st.
If Nature(soueraine misteres ouer wrack)
As thou goest onwards still will plucke thee backe,
She keepes thee to this purpose,that her skill.
May time disgrace,and wretched mynuit kill.
Yet feare her O thou minnion of her pleasure,
She may detaine,but not still keepe her tresure!
Her *Audite*(though delayd)answer'd must be,
And her *Quietus* is to render thee.
  (   )
  (   )

127

IN the ould age blacke was not counted faire,
Or if it weare it bore not beauties name:
But now is blacke beauties successiue heire,
And Beautie slanderd with a bastard shame,
For since each hand hath put on Natures power,
Fairing the foule with Arts fause borrow'd face,
Sweet beauty hath no name no holy boure,
But is prophan'd,if not liues in disgrace.

Therefore my Misterſſe eyes are Rauen blacke,
Her eyes ſo ſuted,and they mourners ſeeme,
At ſuch who not borne faire no beauty lack,
Slandring Creation with a falſe eſteeme,
  Yet ſo they mourne becomming of their woe,
  That euery toung ſaies beauty ſhould looke ſo.

128

HOw oft when thou my muſike muſike playſt,
Vpon that bleſſed wood whoſe motion ſounds
With thy ſweet fingers when thou gently ſwayſt,
The wiry concord that mine eare confounds,
Do I enuie thoſe Iackes that nimble leape,
To kiſſe the tender inward of thy hand,
Whilſt my poore lips which ſhould that harueſt reape,
At the woods bouldnes by thee bluſhing ſtand.
To be ſo tikled they would change their ſtate,
And ſituation with thoſe dancing chips,
Ore whome their fingers walke with gentle gate,
Making dead wood more bleſt then liuing lips,
  Since ſauſie Iackes ſo happy are in this,
  Giue them their fingers,me thy lips to kiſſe.

129

TH'expence of Spirit in a waſte of ſhame
Is luſt in action,and till action , luſt
Is periurd,murdrous,blouddy full of blame,
Sauage,extreame,rude,cruell,not to truſt,
Inioyd no ſooner but diſpiſed ſtraight,
Paſt reaſon hunted, and no ſooner had
Paſt reaſon hated as a ſwollowed bayt,
On purpoſe layd to make the taker mad.
Made In purſut and in poſſeſſion ſo,
Had,hauing,and in queſt,to haue extreame,
A bliſſe in proofe and proud and very wo,
Before a ioy propoſd behind a dreame,
  All this the world well knowes yet none knowes well,
  To ſhun the heauen that leads men to this hell.

130

MY Mistres eyes are nothing like the Sunne,
Currall is farre more red, then her lips red,
If snow be white, why then her brests are dun:
If haires be wiers, black wiers grow on her head:
I haue seene Roses damaskt, red and white,
But no such Roses see I in her cheekes,
And in some perfumes is there more delight,
Then in the breath that from my Mistres reekes.
I loue to heare her speake, yet well I know,
That Musicke hath a farre more pleasing sound:
I graunt I neuer saw a goddesse goe,
My Mistres when shee walkes treads on the ground.
And yet by heauen I thinke my loue as rare,
As any she beli'd with false compare.

131

THou art as tiranous, so as thou art,
As those whose beauties proudly make them cruell;
For well thou know'st to my deare doting hart
Thou art the fairest and most precious Iewell.
Yet in good faith some say that thee behold,
Thy face hath not the power to make loue grone;
To say they erre, I dare not be so bold,
Although I sweare it to my selfe alone.
And to be sure that is not false I sweare
A thousand grones but thinking on thy face,
One on anothers necke do witnesse beare
Thy blacke is fairest in my iudgements place.
In nothing art thou blacke saue in thy deeds,
And thence this slaunder as I thinke proceeds.

132

THine eies I loue, and they as pittying me,
Knowing thy heart torment me with disdaine,
Haue put on black, and louing mourners bee,
Looking with pretty ruth vpon my paine,

And truly not the morning Sun of Heauen
Better becomes the gray cheeks of th' East,
Nor that full Starre that vshers in the Eauen
Doth halfe that glory to the sober West
As those two morning eyes become thy face:
O let it then as well beseeme thy heart
To mourne for me since mourning doth thee grace,
And sute thy pitty like in euery part.
Then will I sweare beauty her selfe is blacke,
And all they foule that thy complexion lacke.

133

BEshrew that heart that makes my heart to groane
For that deepe wound it giues my friend and me;
I'st not ynough to torture me alone,
But slaue to slauery my sweet'st friend must be.
Me from my selfe thy cruell eye hath taken,
And my next selfe thou harder hast ingrossed,
Of him, my selfe, and thee I am forsaken,
A torment thrice three-fold thus to be crossed:
Prison my heart in thy steele bosomes warde,
But then my friends heart let my poore heart bale,
Who ere keepes me, let my heart be his garde,
Thou canst not then vse rigor in my Iaile.
And yet thou wilt, for I being pent in thee,
Perforce am thine and all that is in me.

134

SO now I haue confest that he is thine,
And I my selfe am morgag'd to thy will,
My selfe Ile forfeit, so that other mine,
Thou wilt restore to be my comfort still:
But thou wilt not, nor he will not be free,
For thou art couetous, and he is kinde,
He learnd but suretie-like to write for me,
Vnder that bond that him as fast doth binde.
The statute of thy beauty thou wilt take,
Thou vsurer that put'st forth all to vse,

And

And ſue a friend,came debter for my ſake,
So him I looſe through my vnkinde abuſe.
Him haue I loſt, thou haſt both him and me,
He paies the whole,and yet am I not free.

135

WHo euer hath her wiſh,thou haſt thy *Will*,
And *Will* too boote,and *Will* in ouer-plus,
More then enough am I that vexe thee ſtill,
To thy ſweet will making addition thus.
Wilt thou whoſe will is large and ſpatious,
Not once vouchſafe to hide my will in thine,
Shall will in others ſeeme right gracious,
And in my will no faire acceptance ſhine:
The ſea all water,yet receiues raine ſtill,
And in aboundance addeth to his ſtore,
So thou beeing rich in *Will* adde to thy *Will*,
One will of mine to make thy large *Will* more.
Let no vnkinde,no faire beſeechers kill,
Thinke all but one,and me in that one *Will*.

136

IF thy ſoule check thee that I come ſo neere,
Sweare to thy blind ſoule that I was thy *Will*,
And will thy ſoule knowes is admitted there,
Thus farre for loue, my loue-ſute ſweet fullfill.
Will, will fulfill the treaſure of thy loue,
I fill it full with wils,and my will one,
In things of great receit with eaſe we prooue.
Among a number one is reckon'd none.
Then in the number let me paſſe vntold,
Though in thy ſtores account I one muſt be,
For nothing hold me,ſo it pleaſe thee hold,
That nothing me,a ſome-thing ſweet to thee.
Make but my name thy loue,and loue that ſtill,
And then thou loueſt me for my name is *Will*.

137

THou blinde foole loue,what dooſt thou to mine eyes,

That they behold and see not what they see:
They know what beautie is, see where it lyes,
Yet what the best is, take the worst to be.
If eyes corrupt by ouer-partiall lookes,
Be anchord in the baye where all men ride,
Why of eyes falsehood hast thou forged hookes,
Whereto the iudgement of my heart is tide?
Why should my heart thinke that a seuerall plot,
Which my heart knowes the wide worlds common place?
Or mine eyes seeing this, say this is not
To put faire truth vpon so foule a face,
  In things right true my heart and eyes haue erred,
  And to this false plague are they now transferred.

138

WHen my loue sweares that she is made of truth,
I do beleeue her though I know she lyes,
That she might thinke me some vntuterd youth,
Vnlearned in the worlds false subtilties.
Thus vainely thinking that she thinkes me young,
Although she knowes my dayes are past the best,
Simply I credit her false speaking tongue,
On both sides thus is simple truth suppreſt:
But wherefore sayes she not she is vniust?
And wherefore say not I that I am old?
O loues best habit is in seeming trust,
And age in loue, loues not t'haue yeares told.
  Therefore I lye with her, and she with me,
  And in our faults by lyes we flattered be.

139

O Call not me to iustifie the wrong,
That thy vnkindnesse layes vpon my heart,
Wound me not with thine eye but with thy toung,
Vse power with power, and slay me not by Art,
Tell me thou lou'st else-where; but in my sight,
Deare heart forbeare to glance thine eye aside,
What needst thou wound with cunning when thy might

Is more then my ore-preſt defence can bide?
Let me excuſe thee ah my loue well knowes,
Her prettie lookes haue beene mine enemies,
And therefore from my face ſhe turnes my foes,
That they elſe-where might dart their iniuries:
Yet do not ſo,but ſince I am neere ſlaine,
Kill me out-right with lookes,and rid my paine.

140

BE wiſe as thou art cruell,do not preſſe
My toung-tide patience with too much diſdaine:
Leaſt ſorrow lend me words and words expreſſe,
The manner of my pittie wanting paine.
If I might teach thee witte better it weare,
Though not to loue,yet loue to tell me ſo,
As teſtie ſick-men when their deaths be neere,
No newes but health from their Phiſitions know.
For if I ſhould diſpaire I ſhould grow madde,
And in my madneſſe might ſpeake ill of thee,
Now this ill wreſting world is growne ſo bad,
Madde ſlanderers by madde eares beleeued be.
That I may not be ſo, nor thou be lyde, (wide.
Beare thine eyes ſtraight, though thy proud heart goe

141

IN faith I doe not loue thee with mine eyes,
For they in thee a thouſand errors note,
But 'tis my heart that loues what they diſpiſe,
Who in diſpight of view is pleaſd to dote.
Nor are mine eares with thy toungs tune delighted,
Nor tender feeling to baſe touches prone,
Nor taſte, nor ſmell, deſire to be inuited
To any ſenſuall feaſt with thee alone:
But my fiue wits,nor my fiue ſences can
Diſwade one fooliſh heart from ſeruing thee,
Who leaues vnſwai'd the likeneſſe of a man,
Thy proud hearts ſlaue and vaſſall wretch to be:
Onely my plague thus farre I count my gaine,
That ſhe that makes me ſinne,awards me paine.

142

LOue is my sinne, and thy deare vertue hate,
Hate of my sinne, grounded on sinfull louing,
O but with mine, compare thou thine owne state,
And thou shalt finde it merrits not reproouing,
Or if it do, not from those lips of thine,
That haue prophan'd their scarlet ornaments,
And seald false bonds of loue as oft as mine,
Robd others beds reuenues of their rents.
Be it lawfull I loue thee as thou lou'st those,
Whome thine eyes wooe as mine importune thee,
Roote pittie in thy heart that when it growes,
Thy pitty may deserue to pittied bee.
If thou doost seeke to haue what thou doost hide,
By selfe example mai'st thou be denide.

143

LOe as a carefull huswife runnes to catch,
One of her fethered creatures broake away,
Sets downe her babe and makes all swift dispatch
In pursuit of the thing she would haue stay:
Whilst her neglected child holds her in chace,
Cries to catch her whose busie care is bent,
To follow that which flies before her face:
Not prizing her poore infants discontent;
So runst thou after that which flies from thee,
Whilst I thy babe chace thee a farre behind,
But if thou catch thy hope turne back to me:
And play the mothers part kisse me, be kind.
So will I pray that thou maist haue thy *Will*,
If thou turne back and my loude crying still.

144

TWo loues I haue of comfort and dispaire,
Which like two spirits do sugiest me still,
The better angell is a man right faire:
The worser spirit a woman collour'd il.
To win me soone to hell my femall euill,

Tempteth

Tempteth my better angel from my sight,
And would corrupt my saint to be a diuel:
Wooing his purity with her fowle pride.
And whether that my angel be turn'd finde,
Suspect I may, yet not directly tell,
But being both from me both to each friend,
I gesse one angel in an others hel.
  Yet this shal I nere know but liue in doubt,
  Till my bad angel fire my good one out.

145

THose lips that Loues owne hand did make,
Breath'd forth the sound that said I hate,
To me that languisht for her sake:
But when she saw my wofull state,
Straight in her heart did mercie come,
Chiding that tongue that euer sweet,
Was vsde in giuing gentle dome:
And tought it thus a new to greete:
I hate she alterd with an end,
That follow'd it as gentle day,
Doth follow night who like a fiend
From heauen to hell is flowne away.
  I hate, from hate away she threw,
  And sau'd my life saying not you.

146

POore soule the center of my sinfull earth,
My sinfull earth these rebbell powres that thee array,
Why dost thou pine within and suffer dearth
Painting thy outward walls so costlie gay?
Why so large cost hauing so short a lease,
Dost thou vpon thy fading mansion spend?
Shall wormes inheritors of this excesse,
Eate vp thy charge? is this thy bodies end?
Then soule liue thou vpon thy seruants losse,
And let that pine to aggrauat thy store;
Buy tearmes diuine in selling houres of drosse:

Within be fed, without be rich no more,
So ſhalt thou feed on death,that feeds on men,
And death once dead,ther's no more dying then.

147

MY loue is as a feauer longing ſtill,
For that which longer nurſeth the diſeaſe,
Feeding on that which doth preſerue the ill,
Th'vncertaine ſicklie appetite to pleaſe:
My reaſon the Phiſition to my loue,
Angry that his preſcriptions are not kept
Hath left me,and I deſperate now approoue,
Deſire is death,which Phiſick did except.
Paſt cure I am,now Reaſon is paſt care,
And frantick madde with euer-more vnreſt,
My thoughts and my diſcourſe as mad mens are,
At randon from the truth vainely expreſt.
For I haue ſworne thee faire,and thought thee bright,
Who art as black as hell,as darke as night.

148

O Me! what eyes hath loue put in my head,
Which haue no correſpondence with true ſight,
Or if they haue,where is my iudgment fled,
That cenſures falſely what they ſee aright?
If that be faire whereon my falſe eyes dote,
What meanes the world to ſay it is not ſo?
If it be not,then loue doth well denote,
Loues eye is not ſo true as all mens:no,
How can it? O how can loues eye be true,
That is ſo vext with watching and with teares?
No maruaile then though I miſtake my view,
The ſunne it ſelfe ſees not,till heauen cleeres.
O cunning loue,with teares thou keepſt me blinde,
Leaſt eyes well ſeeing thy foule faults ſhould finde.

149

CAnſt thou O cruell,ſay I loue thee not,
When I againſt my ſelfe with thee pertake:

Doe

Doe I not thinke on thee when I forgot
Am of my selfe, all tirant for thy sake?
Who hateth thee that I doe call my friend,
On whom froun'st thou that I doe faune vpon,
Nay if thou lowrst on me doe I not spend
Reuenge vpon my selfe with present mone?
What merrit do I in my selfe respect,
That is so proude thy seruice to dispise,
When all my best doth worship thy defect,
Commanded by the motion of thine eyes.
But loue hate on for now I know thy minde,
Those that can see thou lou'st,and I am blind.

150

OH from what powre hast thou this powrefull might,
VVith insufficiency my heart to sway,
To make me giue the lie to my true sight,
And swere that brightnesse doth not grace the day?
Whence hast thou this becomming of things il,
That in the very refuse of thy deeds,
There is such strength and warrantise of skill,
That in my minde thy worst all best exceeds?
Who taught thee how to make me loue thee more,
The more I heare and see iust cause of hate,
Oh though I loue what others doe abhor,
VVith others thou shouldst not abhor my state.
If thy vnworthinesse raisd loue in me,
More worthy I to be belou'd of thee.

151

LOue is too young to know what conscience is,
Yet who knowes not conscience is borne of loue,
Then gentle cheater vrge not my amisse,
Least guilty of my faults thy sweet selfe proue.
For thou betraying me, I doe betray
My nobler part to my grose bodies treason,
My soule doth tell my body that he may,
Triumph in loue,flesh staies no farther reason,

But ryſing at thy name doth point out thee,
As his triumphant prize,proud of this pride,
He is contented thy poore drudge to be
To ſtand in thy affaires,fall by thy ſide.
  No want of conſcience hold it that I call,
  Her loue, for whoſe deare loue I riſe and fall.

152

IN louing thee thou know'ſt I am forſworne,
But thou art twice forſworne to me loue ſwearing,
In act thy bed-vow broake and new faith torne,
In vowing new hate after new loue bearing:
But why of two othes breach doe I accuſe thee,
When I breake twenty:I am periur'd moſt,
For all my vowes are othes but to miſuſe thee:
And all my honeſt faith in thee is loſt.
For I haue ſworne deepe othes of thy deepe kindneſſe:
Othes of thy loue,thy truth,thy conſtancie,
And to inlighten thee gaue eyes to blindneſſe,
Or made them ſwere againſt the thing they ſee.
  For I haue ſworne thee faire:more periurde eye,
  To ſwere againſt the truth ſo foule a lie.

153

C*Vpid* laid by his brand and fell a ſleepe,
A maide of *Dyans* this aduantage found,
And his loue-kindling fire did quickly ſteepe
In a could vallie-fountaine of that ground:
Which borrowd from this holie fire of loue,
A dateleſſe liuely heat ſtill to indure,
And grew a ſeething bath which yet men proue,
Againſt ſtrang malladies a ſoueraigne cure:
But at my miſtres eie loues brand new fired,
The boy for triall needes would touch my breſt,
I ſick withall the helpe of bath deſired,
And thether hied a ſad diſtemperd gueſt.
  But found no cure,the bath for my helpe lies,
  Where *Cupid* got new fire;my miſtres eye.

154

154

THe little Loue-God lying once a sleepe,
Laid by his side his heart inflaming brand,
Whilst many Nymphes that vou'd chast life to keep,
Came tripping by, but in her maiden hand,
The fayrest votary tooke vp that fire,
Which many Legions of true hearts had warm'd,
And so the Generall of hot desire,
Was sleeping by a Virgin hand disarm'd.
This brand she quenched in a coole Well by,
Which from loues fire tooke heat perpetuall,
Growing a bath and healthfull remedy,
For men diseasd, but I my Mistrisse thrall,
Came there for cure and this by that I proue,
Loues fire heates water, water cooles not loue.

FINIS.

梁宗岱《莎士比亚十四行选译》

题目与签名为梁宗岱手笔
二十五首译诗由誊抄者书写
使用自印“梁宗岱稿纸”
1956年5月15日随信寄巴金
现藏上海巴金故居

致巴金信及“翻译凡例”文本
见本书前言第XIII-XVI页

莎士比亚十四行选译

梁宗岱

三二

倘你活过我躊躇滿志的大限，
當死那痞子用黃土把我掩埋，
偶然重翻這粗拙可憐的詩卷，
你情人生前寫來献給你的愛，
把它和當代俊逸的新詩相比，
發覺它的詞筆處處都不如人，
請保留它為了我的愛，而不是
為那已被幸運天才凌駕的韻。
呵，那時候就請賜給我這摯思：
「要是我朋友的詩神與時俱長，
他的愛就會帶來更美的產兒，
可以和這世紀的傑作同俯仰；
但他既死去，詩人們又都邁進，
我讀他們的格調，卻讀他的心。」

四。

奪掉我的愛，愛啊，請通通奪去；
看看比你已有的能多些什麼？
沒有愛，愛啊，配得起真愛這字；
我一切早屬你，縱使不添這個。
那麼，倘你為愛我接受我所愛，
我不能責備你把我的愛使用；
但得受責備，如果把自己欺紿，
你由妄念貪嘗你自己所不容。
我可以寬恕你的掠奪，溫柔賊，
雖然你把我僅有的通通偷走；
可是，忍受愛情的暗算，愛曉得，
比憎恨的明傷是更大的煩憂。
　淫靡的嫵媚，連你的惡也嫵媚，
　儘管毒殺我；我們可別相仇視。

四

假如我這笨拙的体質是思想，
不做美的距離就不会阻止我，
因為我就会從那迢迢的遠方，
无論多隔絕，被带到你的寓所。
那麽，縱使我的腿站在那離你
最遠的地角，于我有什麽妨害；
因為空灵的思想超越海和地，
一想去那裡便立刻到達无碍。

但，嘆，思想毒殺我：我並非思想，
去超越遼廓的萬里當你去後；
而且，滿載着泥和水的鈍度裏，
我只好用悲泣去把時光伺候；
這兩种重濁的元素毫无所賜
除掉眼淚，二者的苦惱的標誌。

四五

其餘兩種，輕清的風，淨化的火，
一個是我的思想，一個是慾望，
都是和你一起，無論我居何所；
他們在又不在地神迅地來往。
因為，當這兩种較輕快的元素
帶着愛情的溫柔使命去見你，
我的生命，本賦有四大，只守住
兩個，就不勝其憂鬱，奄奄待斃；
直到生命的結合得完全恢復
由于這兩個敏捷使者的來歸，
他們現正從你那裡回來，欣悉
你起居康吉，在向我殷殷告慰：
　說完了，我樂，可是這並不很久，
　我打發他們囬去，馬上又發愁。

五十

多麽沉重地我在旅途上跋涉，
當我所尋找——我的倦旅的終点——
教那安逸和休憩這樣对我説：
「你又離開了你的朋友那麽遠！」
那馱我的獸，经不起我的憂戚，
馱着我心裡的重負遲遲前進，
彷彿這畜牲由某种本能曉得
他主人不願太快，因離你遠征：
有時惱怒把那血淋淋的靴釘
猛刺他的皮，也不能把他催促；
他只是沉重地报以一声呻吟，
于我，比刺他的靴釘还要尖酷；
因為這呻吟使我省悟和熟筹：
他的憂愁在前面，快樂在後頭。

五一

這樣，我的愛就可原諒那笨獸
（當我離開你）他那遲鈍的冒犯：
從你所在地我何必匆匆地走？
直到我歸來，絕对用不着趕路。
啊，我可憐的畜牲怎会得寬容，
當迅速的極端也要顯得遲鈍？
那時我就要猛刺，縱使在御風，
如飛的速度我只覺得是停頓：
那時就沒有馬能和慾望齊驅；
因此，慾望，由最理想的愛造成，
就引頸長嘶，當他火似地飛馳；
但愛，為了愛，將這樣饒那畜牲：
　既然別你的時候他故意慢走，
　歸途我就要跑步，讓他得自由。

五四

啊，我們会覺得美美得多少倍
由于真所賜她的溫甜的裝璜！
玫瑰花很美，但我們覺得更美
為了她裡面那縷溫甜的芳香。
野薔薇的姿色也是同樣綺旎
比起玫瑰花芳馥四溢的姣顏，
同掛在刺上，同樣会擾首弄姿
當夏天呼息把她的嫩蕊輕展：
但他們唯一的美德只在色相，
開時無人眷戀，萎謝也無人理；
寂寞地死去。香的玫瑰却兩樣；
人把她那馨香的死釀成香液：
　你也如此，美麗而可愛的青春，
　當韶華凋謝，請提取你的純精。

五五

沒有雲石或王公們金的墓碑
能夠和我這些強勁的詩比壽；
你將在這些詩裡彪炳，遠勝于
那被齷齪的時光塗抹的石頭。

當那殘暴的戰爭把石像推翻，
或內訌把城池蕩成一片荒墟，
無論戰神的劍或戰爭的烈燄
都焚不掉你這遺芳的活記載。

衝过死亡和一切善忘的仇恨，
你將昂然走出來；而你的讚美
將永在萬世萬代的眼裡輝映，
直到這世界消耗完了的末日。

這樣，直到最後審判把你喚起，
你活在詩裡，住在情人的眼裡。

六三

像我現在一樣，我的愛將不免
遭時光的毒手所粉碎和消耗，
當時辰吮乾他的血，把他的臉
填滿了縐紋；當他韶年的清朝
已經爬到暮年的巉岩的黑夜，
而他主宰的一切風流和逸韻
都漸漸消滅或已經完全消滅，
偷走了他青春所儲藏的至珍；
為那時候我現在就厲兵秣馬
去抵抗兇暴時光的殘酷利刃，
使他無法把吾愛的芳菲抹煞，
雖則他能夠砍斷吾愛的生命。
　他的美將在這些詩行裡現形，
　它們將長存，而他在裡面長青。

六四

當我眼見前代的富麗和豪華
給時光的手毫不留情地磨滅；
當巍峨的塔我眼見淪為碎瓦，
連永久的銅也不免一場浩刧；

當我眼見那飢餓難填的大海
一步一步把岸上的疆土侵蝕，
汪洋的水又漸漸被陸地主宰，
失既變成了得，得又變成了失；

當我看見了這些擾攘和廢興，
或者連廢興一旦也化為烏有；
毀滅便教我再三這樣地反省：
時光終要跑來把我的愛帶走。

啊，致命的思想！它不得不哀傷
為了它那隨時都可失的珍藏。

既然鋼，或石、或地，或無邊大海，
没有不被那陰慘的無常屈服，
美，她的力量比一朵花還柔脆，
怎能和他那肅殺的嚴威申訴？
呵，夏天温馨的呼息怎能支持
發暴的日子刻刻猛烈的轟炸，
當岩石，無論怎麽險固，或鋼扉，
無論多堅强，都要被時光磨化？

呵，駭人的思想，時光的珍飾，唉，
怎能够不被收進時光的寶箱？
什麽勁手能把他捷足挽回來，
或誰能禁止他把美麗掠搶？
　呵，没有誰，除非這奇蹟有力量：
　我的愛在翰墨裏永久放光芒。

六六

厭了一切，我向安逸的死呼籲，
比方，眼見勳勞生來是叫化子，
和無用的廢物整天逐酒徵歌，
和極純的信義不幸被人背棄，
和金的榮譽被人可耻地誤戴，
和處女美德被人粗暴地玷辱，
和合法的完美被人違法污敗，
和力量被殘缺的權力所屈服，

和愚蠢擺博士架子駕御才能，
和藝術被官府弄得結舌箝口，
和淳厚的真誠被人誤稱愚笨，
和囚徒善得要把統帥惡侍候：
厭了這一切，我要遠遠地逃避，
只是，我一死，吾愛就孤零無依。

我死去的時候別再為我悲哀，
當你聽見那沉重陰慘的葬鐘
普告給全世界說我已經逃開
這齷齪世界去伴最齷齪的蟲；
不呀，當你讀到這詩，別再記起
那寫它的手；因為我愛到這樣，
寧願被遺忘在你甜蜜的心裏，
如果想起了我會使得你哀傷。

哦，如果，我說，如果你看見這詩，
那時候我也許已經化作泥土，
連我這可憐的名字也別提起，
但願你的愛和我的生命同腐。
　生怕這聰明世界猜透你的心，
　在我死去後連你也看作笑柄。

七二

啊，生怕這世界会强逼你自招
我有什麽好處使你在我死後
仍愛我，愛啊，請把我完全忘掉，
因我一点值得你提的都沒有；
除非你揑造出一些美麗的謊
過分為我吹噓我原有的價值，
把瞑目長眠的我阿諛和誇獎，
遠超過鄙吝的事實所願昭示：

啊，怕你的真愛因此顯得虛偽，
怕你為愛的緣故替我說假話，
但願我的名字和我肉体長埋，
以免活下去把你和我都羞煞：
　羞煞我，為了我那可憐的表現；
　羞煞你，為了你那不值的依恋。

七九

當初我獨自向你祈求着協助，
僅我的詩具備你一切的嫵媚；
但現在我清新的節奏既朽腐，
我的病詩神只好給別人讓位。
我承認，愛啊，你這美妙的題材
值得更高明的手筆慘淡经营；
可是你的詩人不过向你还債，
他把奪自你的當作他的发明。
他賜你美德，美德這詞他只從
你的行為偷取；他加給你秀妍，
其实在你頰上找着；他的歌頌
没有一句不是在你身上发見。
　那麽，請别感激他对你的稱讚，
　既然他只把欠你的向你償还。

八二

我承認你沒和我詩神結同心，
因而可以毫無愧赧地去俯覽
詩人獻給你——他們的灵感——的韻：
美麗的灵感，使每首詩增妍！
你的智慧和姿色都一樣出众，
發覺你的價值比我的讚美高，
因此你不得不到別處去追踪
這邁進的時代更生動的寫照。
就這麽辦，愛啊！但當他們已经
使盡了浮誇的辭藻把你刻劃，
真美的你只能由真誠的知音
用真朴的話把你真实地表達；
　他們的濃脂粉只配拿去染紅
　貧血的臉頰；对于你却是濫用。

八三

我從不覺得你需要塗脂盪粉，
因而從不用脂粉塗抹你紅顏；
我發覺，或以為發覺，你的丰韻
遠超出詩人所獻的無謂繾綣：
因此，關于你我的歌只裝睡着，
好讓你自己生動地現身說法，
証明現代的筆桿是多麽粗拙，
要把美德，你裡面的美德增華。
你把我這沈默認為我的罪愆，
其实却應該是我最大的榮光；
因為我的沈默使美絲毫無減，
而別人想活你，却反把你埋葬。
　你任何一隻慧眼所藏的光輝
　都多于你兩詩人所擬的讚美。

八四

誰說得最好，那個說得更圓滿
比起這豐富的讚詞：「只有你是你」？
在這界限裡藏着你全部財產，
你每個平輩都必須和它比擬。
那枝文筆实在是枯瘠得可憐，
如果它不能把題材多少美化；
但誰寫到你，只要他能夠表現
你就是你．他的故事已夠偉大。
讓他只忠实地照你原稿直抄，
別把大自然的玄縫天衣弄壞，
這樣的複本已足顯出他高妙，
使他的風格到處都受人崇拜。
　你將对你美的祝福加上咒詛：
　太愛人讚美，連讚美也受玷污。

八六

是否他那雄渾的詩句，昂昂然
揚帆直駛去征伏太珍貴的你，
使我成熟的思想在腦裡流產，
把孕育它們的胎盤變成墓地？
是否他心灵，從幽灵学会去寫
超凡的警句，把我生生地殛斃？
不呀，既不是他，也不是他那些
黑夜的助手，能使我的詩昏迷。

他，或那個夜夜用靈幻的天才
灌他的親善幽灵都不能誇口
是他們勝利地使我沉默起來；
他們的威脅絕不能使我憂愁：
但如果你的嘉許充滿他的詩，
那我就缺灵感；這才使我頹唐。

八七

别了！你那麼宝貴，那容我占有？
而且顯然你懂得自己的評價：
你價值的証券已够还你自由，
我在你身上的債權通通作罷。
因為沒你批准我怎能占有你？
我又有什麼配得上這樣財宝？
這美好礼物于我既毫无根據，
我專利的执照便不得不取消。

從前你賜我，不曉得自己宝貴，
不然就誤会了我，你的受賜者；
因此，你的大礼物，既出自誤会，
就復歸于你，経过更好的判决。
　這樣，我曾占有你，像一個美梦，
　在梦裡称王，醒來只是一場空。

但你儘不顧一切把自己偷走，
直到生命終点總不免屬于我。
而生命絕不会比愛留得更久，
因它全賴你的愛，無論死或活。
那麼我就不用怕最大的灾害，
既然最小的已足致我于死地。
我看見一個至上的幸福境界，
它並不因你的愛或憎而轉移；

我再也不為你的反覆而頹喪，
既然你一反臉我生命便完畢。
啊，我得到怎樣的幸福的保障，
幸福于你的愛，為它幸福而死！
　但什麼能美滿到不怕受污玷？
你会出賣我，同時还把我瞞騙。

于是我将活下去，認為你忠貞，
像被騙的丈夫；于是愛的面目
对我仍将是愛，雖然已翻了新；
眼睛儘望着我，心兒却在別處；
因為憎恨既不能存在你眼裡，
我又怎能看出你对我的轉变？
对普通人每段假情意的歷史，
都在顰眉，蹙額或氣色上活現，

但上天造你的時候早已註定
溫情要永遠在你的臉上逗留；
不管你的心怎樣变幻无憑準，
你的眼只能訴說旖旎和溫柔。
　你的嫵媚将会像夏娃的蘋果，
　你的美德若不能跟外表配合。

九四

誰有力量傷害人却不願意幹，
誰不做人以為他們愛做的事，
誰感動別人，自己却石頭一樣，
氷冷，去動于中，對誘惑善抗拒，——
他們恰當地承受上天的恩寵，
善于儲藏和保管自然的豐阜；
他們是自己的優美的主人翁，
而不像別人，只能把它們看守。

夏天的花把夏天薰得多芳馥，
雖然對自己它只自開又自落，
但萬一那花受了感染所污毒，
最賤的野草也凌駕它的品格：

因極香的東西腐爛就成極臭，
爛百合花比野草臭得更難受。

我離開你的時候正好是春天，
當錦繡的四月，披上新的光耀，
把活潑的春心給萬物灌注遍，
連沈重的土星也跟着笑和跳。
可是无論鳥的歌，无論那萬紫
千紅和芬芳四溢的栩栩鮮花，
都不能使我訴説夏天的故事，
或着從大地懷裡把它們採擷：
我也不驚羡那百合花的潔白，
也不讚美玫瑰花的深的紅暈；
它們不过是香，是悦目的雕刻，
你才是這一切的模型和真身。
　因此，于我还是嚴冬，而，你不在，
　像逗着你影子我逗它們開懷。

一〇六

當我從那湮遠的古代的紀年
發見那絕代風流人物的寫真，
艷色使得古老的歌詠也香艷，
頌讚着多情騎士和絕命佳人，
于是，從那些国色天姿的描畫，
无論手，或腳，或唇，或眼，或眉額，
我發覺那些古拙的筆所揭發
恰好是你現在所主宰的姿色。

所以他們的讚美无非是預言
我們這時代，一切都預告着你；
不过他們觀察只用想像的眼，
还不够才力把你歌頌得盡致：
　而我們，幸而得親眼看見今天，
　只能用眼讚嘆，却缺舌頭表現。

更觉良工心独苦

——梁宗岱翻译莎士比亚十四行诗纪程

刘志侠

梁宗岱是很多人熟悉的二十世纪翻译家，译作数量不多，但都是精雕细琢的作品，《莎士比亚十四行诗》是其中一种，生命力极强，不受时间的侵蚀，不怕语言的时代嬗变，吸引了一代又一代的读者和研究者。

中学生英语

梁宗岱熟谙法语、德语、意大利语和英语，前三种在 1924 年至 1931 年游学欧洲的七年时期，从 ABC 学起。这时他已超过二十二岁，成年人学外语，起步晚无疑是一种障碍，但他轻易迈过，得到两位法国文学大师不约而同的赞扬：

尽管梁宗岱先生是中国人，并且初习我们的语言，他在诗歌和谈话中，似乎不仅精通，而且热衷于这些相当特殊的精美，运用和谈论起来都出奇地好。（瓦莱里，法译《陶潜诗选》序，1931 年）

他二十四五岁，法语说得很出色，甚至完全没有口音。和欧洲人相比，中国人学习欧洲语言多么容易，尽管他们对我们的一些字母完全陌生，例如 r，但是梁宗岱做到像巴黎人那样以小舌发出颤音。（罗曼·罗兰，日记手稿，1929 年 10 月 17 日）

至于英语，学习背景完全不同。1918 年，十五岁的梁宗岱以新会县立中学一年级肄业的学历，报考广州培正中学，获得录取。但是培正学生从“小学五年级即开始读英文。我不懂英文，只得降级读英文专修科一年才勉强于 1919 年升上中学”（梁宗岱《我的简史》）。当时的学制小学七年，以一年时间补完五至七年级的三年课程，成绩已很骄人，梁宗岱却谦称“勉强”过关，这是因为培正中学虽然与其他中学一样，都属于二十世纪初的“新学”，但英文水平远高于其他中学。

学校创办人是三位浸信会华人医生教友，1889 年成立培正书院，先后聘请了三位美国大学毕业的华人硕士当校长。1926 年以前，教会学校不必向政府立案，培正利用这一特殊条件，在 1916 年开设中学部时，全套照搬美国的中学教育系统：

> 中学部除了国文一科以外，其他各科都用英文教授。中一的教员在初上课还兼用着多少中文解释。到了中二可就不同了，什么都ABC，甚而至教几何画的劳作教员李福耀先生，也得操着英语来教授呢。
>
> 各科（国文除外）所用的课本都是如假包换的舶来品——英美出版物。各教员都很用心地指导。因此那时英文成绩的确过得去。
>
> 然而，环境上的影响还来得大哩：
>
> 在早祷会里，唱诗，祷告，读经，启应，演讲，校务宣传，用的统统是英语；宿舍里有许多房间都贴着“室内谈话，概用英语”的英文标语；课室情形也差不多。违犯了的得纳款一角或半角；就是级社开联欢会，也竟有规定完全用英语的哩。
>
> 在这情况下，筑起了培正英文程度优良的宝塔，高耸在南中国的云霄。（李孟标，《千般感慨话当年》，1939年）

培正中学的毕业证书获得美国教育当局认证，与美国证书等量齐观，毕业生不必通过考试，可以直接入读接受他们的美国大学。

梁宗岱从来没有踏足英国或美国，却年纪轻轻就掌握了英语。当他开始投入新文学运动时，新诗写作与英诗翻译齐头并进，后者甚至赶过前者。1921年，他在全国性刊物发表的第一篇作品不是新诗，是译文，泰戈尔的《他为什么不回来呢？》（《园丁集》第三十六首），刊登在《学生杂志》上，这时离他从字母开始学习英文仅仅三年。

梁宗岱如饥似渴地沉迷在英语书本中。根据他在中学时期所写的文章以及翻译，他至少读过但丁、泰戈尔、华兹华斯、拜伦、雪莱、歌德、惠特曼、朗费罗等古典大家原著或英译本。最令人惊奇的是他连但丁《神曲》这样宏大深奥的著作也不害怕，向一位美国女教师借来阅读，并写下评介文章《檀德及其神曲》，刊《培正青年》二卷九号。

五十多年后，1976年，他的大女儿梁思薇一家人首次自美回国探亲，大女婿齐锡生是旅美的民国史专家，他在一次闲谈中，向我们回忆当时一件事。梁宗岱很高兴看到小外孙女，要为她朗读一首诗歌。他从书架上抽出一本英文书，开始朗诵，一开口整个人好像离开了这个世界，浑然忘我，与诗歌飘然物外，一诗既终，闪光的泪水充满了眼角。齐教授最后赞赏地说：他的英文朗诵那么好，发音准确，抑扬顿挫，充满感情，令人称奇。

完美主义诗译的基石

他本来可以在这条英语翻译平坦大道继续前进，但是1924年游学欧洲，他一下子认识了三种全新的外语世界，每一种都拥有一个庞大的文学宝库，多姿多采，教人流连忘返。1930 年他到德国学习德文，11 月 15 日写信给罗曼·罗兰：

> 大函使我非常高兴，并给我极大勇气。要是我耽搁致谢，那是因为我全身投入学习德国语言，希望两三个月内有足够的知识来应付，尤其不会被阻挡在这个文学收藏的财富之外。我瞥见了那么多好东西，我想一把占为己有！……

他沉迷在这三种语言的文学海洋中，整整七年。1936 年，上海时代出版社印行他的第一本译诗集《一切的顶峰》，内收三十七篇作品，英文作者仅得五首，一首译于出国前的 1923 年，其余四首在 1931 年回国后。换而言之，在欧期间，他把英文完全冷落一旁。

这本诗集打着鲜明的瓦莱里诗论烙印。梁宗岱在序言中，自述他自己三条诗译守则：严格选题，深入理解，译不厌精——“不独一行一行地译，并且一字一字地译，甚至连节奏和用韵也极力模仿原作。”

最后这一条守则直接来自瓦莱里，在 1928 年《保罗·梵乐希先生》一文，梁宗岱引述了梵氏的两段论述：

> 一百个泥像，无论塑得如何完美，总比不上一个差不多那么美丽的石像在我们心灵里所引起的宏

伟的观感。前者比我们还要易朽；后者却比我们耐久一点。我们想象那块云石怎样地和雕刻者抵抗；怎样地不情愿脱离那固结的黑暗。这口，这手臂，都糜费了无数的时日。经过了艺术家几许的匠心……然后才得成这坚固而柔媚的精灵，在无定的期间从同样坚贞的思想产生出来的。

接受了这些格律之后，我们便不能什么都干了；我们便不能什么都说了……只有上帝才有思行合一的特权。我们呢，我们是要劳苦的；我们是要很苦闷地感到思想与实现底区分的。我们要追寻不常有的字，和不可思议的偶合；我们要在无力里挣扎，尝试着音与义底配合，要在光天化日中创造一个使做梦的人精力俱疲的梦魇……（《关于阿都尼》）

梁宗岱据此作出结论：

诗，最高的文学，遂不能不自己铸些镣铐，做它所占有的容易的代价。这些无理的格律，这些自作孽的桎梏，就是赐给那松散的文字一种抵抗性的；对于字匠，它们替代了云石底坚固，强逼他去制胜，强逼他去解脱那过于散漫的放纵的。

这是一种完美主义的诗译，是他终生追求的目标。

1935年，梁宗岱与沉樱自日本归国，次年被聘请为天津南开大学英文系教授，系主任柳无忌回忆道：

> 当时有一点踌躇，不知道那位新教授在上课时用英文演讲，有无困难。出乎我意料之外，宗岱的英文相当通畅，加上他的学识、才气，他在教书时的用功与认真，以及他那股待人接物的热情与做事的劲儿，他的参加增强了我们英文系的阵容。（《才华横溢的诗人——梁宗岱教授》）

系里专门为梁宗岱增设新课程“西洋文学名著选读”，由他演讲及安排系内教授参加，就这样，梁宗岱重新和英文接回轨道。

在南开大学任教前，1935年11月8日，天津《大公报》副刊创立《诗特刊》，每星期一期，交给梁宗岱担任主编。他以一篇《新诗底十字路口》（入集《诗与真二集》时更名《新诗底纷歧路口》）作为发刊词，参照西洋诗的发展历史，认为新文学的新诗已经完成萌芽初期的自由诗阶段，必须寻求新的路径提升和发展。他从瓦莱里诗歌理论出发，提议讨论一个重要的基本问题，“发见新音节和创造新格律”（后简称“创格”）。

文章引起巨大的反响，沈从文第一个以长文回应，接着来自四面八方的诗人、作家和文艺理论家争相加入讨论，一时间，《诗特刊》变成一个纸上文学沙龙和写作坊。既展示长篇大论的各家之言，又陈列珠玉纷呈的实验性诗篇。讨论很快溢出《大公报》，入侵其他文艺刊物，持续超过一年半时间，直到1937年中日战争爆发，《大公报》南迁才停止。梁宗岱推动的这场“创格”运动是中国现代文学史上一场重要的辩论，最后在文学界达成一种共识：新诗和古典诗歌一样，需要接受形式和格律的束缚，中国新诗必须走出自由诗，步向更高阶段。

走进莎士比亚花园

在这种热烈的讨论氛围中，梁宗岱与其他诗人都尝试在写作中实验“创格”，他挑选的对象是外国诗中译——莎士比亚十四行诗。

最早的成果发表在1937年6月上海《文学杂志》一卷二期上，第三十三首和第六十五首。采用每行十二字格律，一行五音步（当时也称为音组、音尺、拍、顿、音顿、音节、节奏……），每个音步由一至四字组成。

梁宗岱一直不喜欢把Sonnet译为“十四行诗”，直到五十年代仍使用旧名“商籁”。杂志主编朱光潜选用《莎士比亚十四行诗两首》作总题，这是他的主编权力，也因为他是梁宗岱在法国结识的知心朋友，“一位我所钦佩的且愈打愈成交的老友”（朱光潜《论直觉与表现答难》，

1945 年）。朱光潜积极参加《大公报》的新诗格律讨论，写过多篇文章，他把这种友好切磋的气氛带进自己的刊物，在梁宗岱第三十三首译文后面加上一条“编者附注”：

> 末行原文为 Suns of world may stain when heaven's sun staineth。译文省去前半，如将后二句译为：
>
> 我底爱却不因此向他白眼，
> 人间太阳会失色，天日还常暗。
>
> 似与原文语气较合。　　编者附注。

编者挑剔作者文章，殊为罕见。但梁宗岱毫不介意，同时把这些话挂在心里，二十年多后在香港《文汇报》第三次刊登译文时，这两句诗已经改为：

> 我的爱却并不因此把他鄙贱，
> 天上的太阳有瑕疵，何况人间！

虚己受人，不以人言为忤，千锤百炼，只有对文学忠诚的有道者才会这样做

诗歌发表后一个月，七七事变，梁宗岱踏上流亡道路，经广东到广西。1938 年秋转往重庆，进入上海迁移来的复旦大学外语系，教授英语。在这段流离颠沛的日子里，他没有停止翻译工作。

戴望舒在1938年5月流亡到香港，受聘《星岛日报》筹组副刊《星座》，梁宗岱是他的第一批特约撰稿人，他交出莎氏十四行诗译五首，以总题《商籁五首》在10月13日发表。

一年之后，1939年12月18日，重庆《时事新报》副刊《学灯》以全版篇幅，刊登了他的十首莎氏十四行诗译，前面冠以导言《莎士比亚底商籁》，表示他将系统介绍全部诗作。副刊主编宗白华知道这些诗译的重要性，特别写了一段《编辑后语》推荐：

> 莎士比亚是个“世界的眼睛”，超然地停留在这万千形象之上，把它们摩挲而雕塑出来，轮廓清楚像强烈的日光，而态度的幽冷却像一无情的月亮。
>
> 所以人们都想窥探这冷静的“世界眼睛”背后那颗深秘的心。诗人本当把这颗心完全保留着为他自己的——使他成为世界上最客观的诗人——不幸他对于他的一位年青貌美的朋友和一位“暗色的夫人”热挚的情感终于使他忍俊不禁，写出了他的“商籁”。这些商籁使我们窥见人间最不容易窥见的心，而莎士比亚更可爱了。
>
> 梁先生的译诗亦复可爱：
>
> “只要一天有人类，或人有眼睛，
> 这诗将长存，并且赐给你生命。”

三星期后，1940 年 1 月 15 日，该报再次刊登梁宗岱六首诗译，宗白华在《编辑后语》写道：

> 西洋商籁本就难译成中文体“商籁”，莎翁此作更是不好译，英文原诗也不易尽懂，梁先生准备将莎翁商籁全部一百五十四首译出。本刊六十四期所发表数首内有几个错字，梁先生另又修正了几处，兹列一勘误表于后：

勘误表密密麻麻一长串，除了误排六处，还有译者修订三处，其中第十九首有一句全句改译，“等我躺倒后再来结果一抛”，改为“不要突然走来作事后的摧毁”。刊登后立即作出的修改不仅数量多，而且变化大，显示这些仍是未定稿，有待推敲琢磨，完美主义翻译不是儿戏，要求付出巨大的劳动。

在《学灯》之后，要等到 1943 年 8 月，才再次看到梁译莎诗在刊物上发表。新创刊的《民族文学》从一卷二期开始连载他的翻译。译者再次把《学灯》的导言放在最前面，诗译从第一首开始，顺次序排列。主编陈铨在《编者漫记》中说：

> 八年以前，梁宗岱先生从天津到清华园来，同我谈了一天一夜，袋子里就掏出了翻译的几首莎士比亚的商籁给我看。在这八年中间，经过无量数的

修改，审试，最后才决定在本刊全部发表。像梁先生天资那样高，文字技术那样精的人，却肯这样埋头苦炼，这当然因为原著在世界文学上崇高的价值。这和时下一些以草率迅速，而自翔天才的廉价世界名著介绍者，作风大不相同。

八年前就是1936年，陈铨刚提升为清华大学外文系教授，这段话证实了梁宗岱翻译全部莎氏十四行诗的计划，与他在《大公报·诗特刊》推动“创格”讨论同一时间。他的翻译既得益于讨论者提供的各种意见，也给讨论带来具体的成果。陈铨打算发表全译，可是连载三期后，《民族文学》遽然停刊，只刊登了前面第一至第三十首。过了一年，1944年12月，第三十一至第四十一首在《时与潮文艺》露面，文末编者说明：“（注）第一至三十首在《民族文艺［学］》第二三四期登载”，表示稿件继承自《民族文学》。

不久之后，梁宗岱翻译的歌德《浮士德》开始出现在其他刊物上，再没有见到新的莎氏诗译，可见工作已经暂停。除了这批四十一首外，还有零散发表的九首，已完成而未发表的数量则无法知道。

给巴金的信

1948年后，梁宗岱蛰居广西百色，转向草药研究和提炼，再没有发表文学作品。1952年9月被诬入狱，1954年6月平反释放，根据他本人意愿，安排在南宁市广西省人民医院继续新药实验。两年后，由于研究受阻，他寻求转换工作，首先想到写作和翻译，这是他的本行，而且在文学界有不少好朋友，其中一位是巴金。周立民是巴金专家，目前负责上海巴金故居事务，本节使用的相关文献及资料由他热心提供。

巴金故居收藏的信函中，有一封梁宗岱1956年5月15日来函：

巴金：真正久违了！我［19］51年秋被人诬陷，坐了两年多的牢。幸政府查明，于［19］54年夏恢复自由，旋又恢复省政协委员职。我出狱后，即来广西省人民医院实验我创制的两种新药。该两种药已初步证实可以解决现代医学所不能或很难解决的重病。兹夹上说明书，当略知一二。现广东省人民医院正在实验中。一俟再观察一个时期，即可正式公布。

临床实验之暇，我也抽一部分时间做文学工作。除继续从前的莎氏十四行的翻译外（现已译得106首），还计划较有系统选译雨果的诗，特别是那些富于革命和社会思想的。兹将一部分莎氏十四行和已整理好（注释好）的一首雨果诗的拙译寄上，你看要得吗？浮士德下卷我也打算在短期内译完十四行后开始。可惜我明天要赴百色专区视察，又要耽误不少日子。

夹上省政协委会的信，目的在释疑，非为别的也。

敬礼！

宗岱　[19] 56. 5. 15 日

住址：广西南宁市广西省人民医院第一宿舍

这是一封令人唏嘘的信，两位老朋友中断信息二十多年后重新联络，本应是一件快乐的事情，但是梁宗岱却“夹上省政协委会的信，目的在释疑”。可能他担心对方还不知道他已恢复清白之身，而此信的目的性十分明确，以婉转口气，请求老朋友帮忙出版译作。

他在信中谈到雨果和浮士德，但重点放在“莎氏十四行”，特别选出二十五首，请人以原稿纸誊抄，寄给巴金作样板。其中第三十二首与第四十首曾在 1943 年发表过，他只把三个“底”字改为“的”，没有作其他修订。鉴于这个时期他的经历，这批译作当属 1943 年以前已完成的部分，总数一百零六首。

译稿附有两页亲笔书写的“《莎士比亚十四行》翻译凡例”：

一、意义以直译为主。但亦偶有因语法、语气、节奏或者音韵的需要而略加补充或变通之处，如

我的病诗神〔只好〕给别人让位（七九首）

“只好”是原文所没有的，但译文里没有它则语气和节奏都似欠圆满。

二、形式力求接近原作。不独行数、节拍和韵谱（Rhyme-scheme）完全依照原作，就是原作的双声叠韵也尽可能在译文里模仿出来，如

　　夺掉我的爱，爱啊，请通通夺去，

　　看看比你已有的能多些什么……

一节就是想翻印原作全节以 all、more 等的 O 音为基调的；又如

　　当你听见那沉重阴惨的葬钟

下半行的双声叠韵就是想重现原文的下半行 the surly solemn bell 的 S 和 L 的两重双声的；而

　　烂百合花比野草臭得更难受

则企图以“臭”和“受”的叠韵来替代原作

　　Lilies that fester smell far worse than weeds

里的 worse 和 weeds 的双声，而产生同样的效果。

三、每国诗都有它的“主诗行”（Staple line）。希腊是 Hexameter（六音步诗行），法国是 Alexandrine（十二音诗行），英国是十音五音步或五拍诗行（Decasyllabic）。我国古诗则在不同时期以四言、五言或七言为主。在这些翻译的习作里，我尝试，根据我所了解的语体文的固有音乐性，去融合法国的十二音诗行和英文的五拍诗行为一体而建立一种十二音五拍的诗行，故大部分诗行均系

十二言五拍。如

当死—那痞子—用黄土—把我—掩埋

或

艳色—使得—古老—的歌咏—也香艳等。

但亦有十二言四拍的如

为什么—我的诗—那么缺—新光彩

或十二言六拍的如

其余—两种—轻清—的风—净化—的火。

但这些都是变格，是极少数的例外。

“凡例”是预先制订出来的写作格式及规矩，作为规定去执行。可是他正在寻求发表这批作品，挑出自己认为最出色的诗句作为例子，旁人读起来会觉得他在自我表现。实际上，他在公开自己的翻译秘诀，这是他的经验之谈，无论专业或业余译者，依照他的“凡例”去细读他的例句，都能从中找到有益的启发。

七个例子都是译者满意的诗句，但像其他译文一样，其中三句不是最后版本，后来又作修改，这种译不厌精、追求完美的精神，贯彻在梁宗岱所有翻译中。

香港《文汇报》全译版

梁宗岱在窘境中写信向巴金求援，没有抱太大希望，信发出后不到一个月，没有等到回信便与家人离开南宁，前往广州寻找工作。当时的就业由政府统一管理，他知道希望甚微，却没有料到，命运为他准备了一个大惊喜。罗念生，另一位文友，已经为他在广州找到一份理想的工作。罗念生是希腊文学专家，在《大公报》1936 年新诗格律讨论时与梁宗岱因为辩论而成为好朋友。当梁宗岱落魄广西的时候，他正在中国科学院外国文学研究所任职，有一个令人羡慕的教授职称。1956 年，广州中山大学外语系筹设法文和德文新专业，写信到各地找寻教师，罗念生收到相关询问信件，回信推荐梁宗岱，立即得到校方同意，梁宗岱到广州十多天，出乎意外收到广西的电报通知，要他立即去中山大学报到。

就这样，他不仅重获教授衔头，重登教坛，而且重回一个熟悉的地方，中山大学所在地是他当年念书的岭南大学原址。安顿下来后，他迅速恢复文学创作，一年之后，1957 年，他的布莱克诗译首先在香港《文汇报》连载，先后四次，共二十三首。其他译作、诗词和文艺评论随后而至，陆续出现在本地报刊上。

1962 年是他的创作高峰期，完成《蒙田试笔》的译稿超过二十万字，同时翻译《浮士德》，就在此时，他接到罗念生一封来信，索取莎士比亚十四行诗的译稿。二十多年后，罗念生在《有关梁宗岱的资料》（1988 年）一文中，揭示了这件事的缘起："1962 年，人民文学出版社郑效洵同志要我用个人名义向宗岱索取他翻译的莎士比亚十四行诗。"这是因为 1964 年是莎士比亚诞生四百周年，人文社准备以朱生豪译集作基础，出版一套高质量的《莎士比亚全集》作为纪念。其中的十四行诗，当时只有一本屠岸的全译本，1950 年发表，独占文坛十多年。梁宗岱在战火纷飞的抗战时期发表了四十一首，虽不完整，但数量已排第二位。郑效洵是副总编辑，比较两部作品是份内工作。他请罗念生出面与梁宗岱打交道，结果如何都不会伤和气，处理手法的确高明。

罗念生不知道其中内幕，当人文社决定采用梁译时，他十分惊讶。“我要来以后，人文社把全部十四行诗编入莎士比亚全集。我于 1963 年把译稿带到大连去修改。我曾写信告诉宗岱，他若接受一个字，我就满意了。结果，他全部接受了。”罗念生的表现如此兴奋，好像他就是十四行诗的译者。

梁宗岱的兴奋当然不亚于罗念生，他立即放下其他工作，全力修改及完成十四行诗的翻译。同时把消息与所有朋友分享，包括远在法国的女作家奥克莱（Marcelle Auclair），他们别离三十多年后，刚刚重新联系上，“他的信有一句附言：‘我刚把莎士比亚十四行诗译成中文。’”（奥克莱母女《对话回忆录》，1978 年）

成果很快出来，1963 年 5 月 1 日，第一批译诗刊登在香港《文汇报》副刊《文艺》上，前面有一段简短的编者按语：

明年是莎士比亚诞生四百周年，梁宗岱先生应北京人民文学出版社之请，重译《莎士比亚十四行诗集》准备出书。全部共一百五十四首，《文艺》将陆续优先发表。

连载分三十二期，至次年3月18日顺利刊完。按计划，人文社的《莎士比亚全集》此时已经排版就绪，但到了最后一刻突然生变，取消付印，全部封存，没有人知道其中原因。十年“文革”结束后，拨乱反正，《莎士比亚全集》立即启封，在1978年出版。梁宗岱的十四行诗放在第十一卷，也就是最末一卷，卷目录未署译者名字，翻到作品标题下才能见到。随后几年，这套全集不断重印，四年间印数超过二十万套。

甘少苏《宗岱和我》记载了这次诗集出版经过，“这年［1976年］宗岱已经73岁了……将全部精力投入到翻译工作上。开始重译《莎士比亚十四行诗》，他一鼓作气，只几个月就译完了。”香港《文汇报》曾刊登了梁宗岱的全译，即使手稿在“文革”中被焚，也毋须从零开始，而且没有可能在数月内完成。实际上，文中所说的“重译”应为“重新修订”。这次修订规模之大，教人拍案称奇。一百五十四首诗，改动了一百五十四首，无一例外。

1983年，梁宗岱去世后，远适美国的沉樱女史委托女作家林海音在台北出版此书繁体字版，1992年由纯文学出版社印行，书名《莎士比亚十四行诗》，内文采用人文社版，出版社邀请诗人余光中写了一篇序言《锈锁难开的金钥匙》。

“所入颇深，所出也颇纯”

自从人文社版《莎士比亚全集》面世后，出现一股莎士比亚十四行诗出版热潮，全译本从两种一下子增加十余种，从格律诗体到散文诗体，从文言文到套用前人的诗句，多姿多彩。梁宗岱的译作处身其中，不仅没有显得陈旧过时，反而更突出其现代性和文学光彩。

梁宗岱从不把已发表的译文作为定译，无论是否出版单行本或在报刊发表，只要有机会便重新修改。他发表过的莎氏十四行诗译文可粗分三个版本：1943 年版（文学杂志、学灯、民族文学、时与潮文艺、巴金故居版）、1963 年版（香港文汇版）和 1978 年版（北京人文社版）。前后近四十年，每次都是全面修订，幅度相当大，令译文更臻完美。

试举两个例子。第二十四首第五、六句，三次发表，三次译文不同：

For through the painter must you see his skill,
To find where your true image pictur'd lies,

你得要看进你那画家底身内
去发见他底技巧和你底肖像；（1943 年版）

你要从他身上认识他的艺术，
去发见你的肖像珍藏的地方；（1963 年版）

你要透过画家的巧妙去发见
那珍藏你的奕奕真容的地方；（1978 年版）

第九十七首是另一个例子：

1963年版	1978年版
触目是寒冬的十二月的荒凉！	触目是龙钟腊月的一片萧索！
可是这别离的时期正当盛夏；	可是别离的时期恰好是夏日；
和那丰饶的秋天，孕育着新收，	和膨胀着累累的丰收的秋天，
给青春的淫荡的负担所坠压，	满载着青春的淫荡结下的果实，
像寡妇的妊娠在她良人死后：	好像怀胎的新寡妇，大腹便便：
但这累累的丰富于我只能有	但是这累累的丰收，在我看来，
做孤儿和无父的果实的希望；	只能成无父孤儿和乖异的果；

当然，梁宗岱的译文整体从初刊便已是相当成熟的译作，整首重译的情况不多，字斟句酌的推敲却随处可见。所得的结果是意义表达更为精确，译文的句法和词语追随汉语的时代变化，加上原有的优点，令译文熠熠如新，一尘不染。

我们从1999年开始整理梁宗岱作品，《梁宗岱文集》（2003年）和《梁宗岱著译精华》（2006年）收入的《莎士比亚十四行诗》，采用1978年人文社版，因为这是一家受人信任的出版社。到了2016年编辑《梁宗岱译集》七卷本时，我们设法找到台北纯文学版作参考。余光中是该书序言《锈锁难开的金钥匙》的作者，他的序言是一篇学院派文章，对梁宗岱的翻译给予很高评价，“译笔兼顾了畅达与风雅，看得出所入颇深，所出也颇纯，在莎翁商籁的中译上，自有其正面的贡献”。该书编辑在封底作品简介写道：“诗人余光中誉为十四行诗的最佳翻译！”但没有交代这个称誉的出处。我们特别留意余光中的点评，尤其第二首的两个句子，“诠释欠妥”，也就是“理解错误”：

To say, within thine own deep sunken eyes,
Were an all-eating shame, and thriftless praise.
你说，“在我这双深陷的眼眶里，
是贪婪的羞耻，和无益的颂扬。”

余光中认为梁宗岱没有读通英文原文，“这么一来，文法就不通了，不但语气未完，文意不贴，而且 an all-eating shame and thriftless praise 如何能用 were 做动词呢？”他说得有道理，但错怪了人，因为他没有读过1943年和1963年两个版本，不知道梁宗岱的理解就是他的理解：

> 你回答，“在我这双深陷的眼里”，
> 是难咽的耻辱，和浪费的颂扬。（1943 年版）

> 你回答，“在我这双深陷的眼窝”，
> 是难咽的耻辱，和浪费的颂扬。（1963 年版）

问题出在小小的后引号，人文社版误把位置调后了一行，导致意义全非。既然 1943 年和 1963 年都译对了，不可能到 1978 年才改是成非。很明显是排版时出了岔子，逃过校对者的眼睛。

这件事挑起我们的记忆，1978 年是一个不寻常的年份，百废待举，人才难得，出版工作远未恢复正常，大家一股热情地工作，追赶失去的时光，书籍中出现一些罕见的错误是可以理解的。有鉴于此，我们校订时特别小心，仍然以人文社 1978 年版作为蓝本，因为该版使用梁宗岱生前亲自厘定的译稿，最为可靠，同时参照 1963 年香港《文汇报》连载版和英文原文，以订正出版过程可能出现的人为错误，尤其错漏字和标点。

梁宗岱《莎士比亚十四行诗》是一部成功的译作。他本身是诗人，对诗歌语言有极为敏感的领悟。他采用直译方法，行数、节拍和韵谱力求接近原作，用字典雅而不陈旧，每行十二字的工整格式，带来与中国古诗同样的视觉美感，诗句极具音乐感，五音步的音调悠扬，节奏鲜明多变。

这本书的翻译，让他实现了在《一切的峰顶》序言里的一个梦想：

> 有时候——虽然这也许是千载难逢的——作品在译者心里唤起的回响是那么深沉和清澈，反映在作品里的作者和译者底心灵那么融洽无间，二者底艺术手腕又那么旗鼓相当，译者简直觉得作者是自己前身，自己是作者再世，因而用了无上的热忱、挚爱和虔诚去竭力追摹和活现原作底神采。

是的，梁宗岱把莎士比亚十四行诗成功移植到中文，他的诗译栩栩活现了原作的形神，为中国的文化宝库增添了一笔财富。

2023 年 9 月，巴黎

莎士比亚的商籁[1]

梁宗岱

谁想知道我对于你是朋友还是情人，让他读莎士比亚的商籁，从那里取得一块磨砺他们那只能撕而不能斩的钝质的砥石。

——雪莱

莎士比亚底《商籁集》久为欧洲一般莎士比亚专家聚讼的中心。由于初版底印行完全出于一个盗窃的出版家底贪心和恶意，未经作者手订，便遗下许多难解的纠纷。我们无从确知这些商籁是甚么时候作的，它们的对象是些甚么人，它们最初的出版家在那谜一般的献词里所称的 Mr. W. H. 究竟是谁，诗人在其中几首所提到的敌手是

① 商籁 通译十四行诗。（本书注解除特别说明外，均为编者所加）

哪一个，以及它们底次序和作者原来的次序是否一致等等。连篇累牍的，几乎可以说汗牛充栋的辩论便从此发生了。

这辩论自然有它的兴味，特别是对于有考据癖的人；但这兴味，我以为，不独与诗的价值无关，也许反有妨碍。从纯粹欣赏的观点看来，值得我们深究的，只有一个范围比较广泛，直接系于文艺创作的问题，就是，这些商籁所表现的是诗人的实录呢，抑或只是一些技巧上的表演？

诗人华慈渥斯在一八一五年所作的“抒情小曲自序补遗”里的意见似乎是前一派主张底滥觞，他那首《咏商籁》的商籁里这句诗：

……………

用这条钥匙

莎士比亚打开他的心……

是他们所乐于征引的。“打开他的心”，就是说，诉说他底衷曲，对于许多考据家，就无异于纪录他自己亲切的经验。

于是他们便在这一百五十四首“商籁”里发见许多自传的元素，或者简直是一种自传，一出亲密的喜剧，一部情史，可以增加我们对于这位大诗人底生平现有的简略的认识。他们那么急于证实他们的原理，那么渴望去更清楚认识他们所崇拜的大诗人的面目，以致诗中许多当时流行的辞藻和抒情的意象都被穿凿附会为诗人事迹或遭遇的纪实了。

另一派学者或批评家，根据当时多数诗人都多少直接或间接受意大利诗人培特拉卡底影响而作“商籁环”或“商籁连锁”的风气，却主张莎士比亚不过和其他同时代的诗人一样，把商籁当作一种训练技巧的工具，或藉以获得诗人的荣衔而已。依照这派的说法，他的商籁完全是“非个人的”；它们的主题固是同时代一般商籁的主题；所用的辞藻和意象，也是当代流行的辞藻和意象。莎士比亚并没有渗入他自己亲切的东西，情或意；他不过比同时代许多诗人把那些主题运用得更巧妙，把那些辞藻和意象安排得更恰当更和谐罢了。这一派也有一位诗人做他们底总发言人。白浪宁在他一首诗里反驳华兹渥斯说：

“……用这条钥匙，
莎士比亚打开他的心”——真的吗？
如果是，他就不像莎士比亚！

这反驳在另一位大诗人史文朋的文章里又引起强烈的抗议：“并没有一点不像莎士比亚，但无疑地最不像白浪宁。”

究竟哪一说对呢？这些商籁果真是这位大诗人私生活的实录，所以每个比喻，每个意象都隐含着关于作者的一段逸事，一件史实吗？抑或只是一些流行的主题的游戏，一些技巧上惊人的表演，丝毫没有作者个人底反映呢？

和大多数各走极端的辩论一样，真理似乎恰在二者的中间。

诗人济慈在他一八一七年十月二十二日的一封信里曾经有过这样的话：

> 我身边三部书之一是莎士比亚的诗。我从不曾在“商籁”里发见过这许多美。——我觉得它们充满了无意中说出来的美妙的东西，由于惨淡经营一些诗意的结果。

这段话，骤看似乎全是援助“纯艺术”派，而且曾被其中一个中坚分子 Sir Sidney Lee[①]用来支持他的主张的，其实正足以带我们到这两派中间的接触点。

“无意中说出来”，“惨淡经营一些诗意”，不错。但这些诗意，济慈并没有提及从哪里取来：从柏拉图，从但丁，从培特拉卡，从龙沙？从同时代的商籁作者，还是从他自己的心，从他那多才的丰富的人的经验呢？如果伟大天才的一个特徵，是他的借贷或挹注的能力，我们简直可以说，天才的伟大与这能力适成正比例，所以第一流作家对于宇宙间的一切——无论天然的或人为的——都随意予取予携（歌德关于他的《浮士德》说：“从生活或从书本取来，并无甚关系。”）；那么，他们会舍近求远，只知寻摘搜索于外，而忽略了自己里面那无尽藏的亲切的资源，那唯一足以化一切外来的元素为自

① 西尼·李爵士（Sir Sidney Lee，1859—1926），英国历史学家。

已血肉的创造的源泉吗？

可是要弄清楚。利用自己里面的资源，或者，即如华兹渥斯所说“打开他的心”，在诗的微妙点金术里，和自传是截然两事，没有丝毫共连点的。要想根据诗人的天才的化炼和结晶，重织作者某段生命的节目，在那里面认出一些个别的音容，一些熟悉的名字，实在是“可怜无补费精神”的事。这不独因为对于一个像他那样伟大的天才，私人的遭遇往往具有普遍的意义，他所身受的祸福不仅是个别的孤立的祸福，而是藉他的苦乐显现出来的生命品质。也因为他具有那无上的天赋，把他的悲观的刹那凝成永在的清歌，在那里，像在一切伟大的艺术品里，作者的情感扩大，升华到一个那么崇高、那么精深的程度，以致和它们卑微的本原完全不相属，完全失掉等量了。

从商籁的体裁上说，莎士比亚所采用并奠定的英国式显然是一种无可奈何的变通办法？由于英文诗韵之贫乏，或者也由于英国人的音乐感觉没有那么复杂（英国的音乐比较其他欧洲诸国都落后便是一个明证）。因此，它不独缺乏意大利式商籁的谨严，并且，从严格的诗学家看来，失掉商籁体的存在理由的。但这有甚么关系？就是用这体裁莎士比亚赐给我们一个温婉的音乐和鲜明的意象的宝库，在这里面他用主观的方式完成他在戏剧里用客观的方式所完成的，把镜子举给自然和人看，让德性和热情体认它们自己的面目：让时光照见他自己的形相和印痕；时光，他所带来的妩媚的荣光和衰败的惆怅……对着这样的诗，译者除了要频频辍笔兴叹外，还有甚么可说呢？

初刊1943年8月《民族文学》一卷二期

SHAKESPEARE'S SONNETS

莎士比亚十四行诗

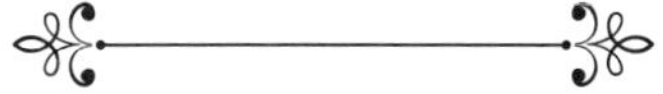

献给下面刊行的十四行诗

唯一的促成者

W.H.先生

祝他享有一切幸运，并希望

我们永生的诗人

所预示的

不朽

得以实现。

对他怀着好意

并断然予以

出版的

T.T.

一

对天生的尤物我们要求蕃盛，
以便[1]美的玫瑰永远不会枯死，
但开透的花朵既要及时凋零[2]，
就应把记忆交给娇嫩的后嗣；
但你，只和你自己的明眸定情，
把自己当燃料喂养眼中的火焰，
和自己作对，待自己未免太狠，
把一片丰沃的土地变成荒田。
你现在是大地的清新的点缀，
又是锦绣阳春的唯一的前锋，
为什么把富源葬送在嫩蕊里，
温柔的鄙夫，要吝啬，反而浪用？
　　可怜这个世界吧，要不然，贪夫，
　　就吞噬世界的份，由你和坟墓。

---

① 以便　文汇报版译文“以使”。
② 凋　“凋”是1955年第一批异体字之一，人文社版按规定使用规范字代替，因此出现雕零、雕残、雕落、雕谢等词组，受类似影响的还有销毁（消毁）和勾销（勾消）等。1988年《现代汉语通用字表》发布后，这些规定已更改。本书根据文汇报版，全面恢复译者原用的词组，不另说明。

二

当四十个冬天围攻你的朱颜，
在你美的园地挖下深的战壕，
你青春的华服，那么被人艳羡，
将成褴褛的败絮，谁也不要瞧：
那时人若问起你的美在何处，
哪里是你那少壮年华的宝藏，
你说，“在我这双深陷的眼眶里”，[①]
是贪婪的羞耻，和无益的颂扬。
你的美的用途会更值得赞美，
如果你能够说，“我这宁馨小童
将总结我的账，宽恕我的老迈”，[②]
证实他的美在继承你的血统！
　　这将使你在衰老的暮年更生，
　　并使你垂冷的血液感到重温。

① 本行与下一行原刊：
　你说，“在我这双深陷的眼眶里，
　是贪婪的羞耻，和无益的颂扬。”
后引号误植后一行，引起歧义。据文汇报版订正。
② 本行末标点按文汇报版订正。

三

照照镜子，告诉你镜中[1]的脸庞，
说现在这庞儿应该另造一副；
如果你不赶快为它重修殿堂，
就欺骗世界，剥掉母亲的幸福。
因为哪里会有女人那么淑贞
她那处女的胎不愿被你耕种？
哪里有男人那么蠢，他竟甘心
做自己的坟墓，绝自己的血统？
你是你母亲的镜子，在你里面
她唤回她的盛年的芳菲四月：
同样，从你暮年的窗你将眺见——
纵皱纹满脸——你这黄金的岁月。
　　但是你活着若不愿被人惦记，
　　就独自死去，你的肖像和你一起。

① 你镜中　原刊“你那镜中”，据文汇报版修订。

四

俊俏的浪子，为什么把你那份
美的遗产在你自己身上耗尽？
造化的馈赠非赐予，她只出赁；
她慷慨，只赁给宽宏大量的人。
那么，美丽的鄙夫，为什么滥用
那交给[①]你转交给别人的厚礼？
赔本的高利贷者，为什么浪用
那么一笔大款，还不能过日子？
因为你既然只和自己做买卖，
就等于欺骗你那妩媚的自我。
这样，你将拿什么账目去交代，
当造化唤你回到她怀里长卧？
　　你未用过的美将同你进坟墓；
　　用呢，就活着去执行你的遗嘱。

① 交给　文汇报版为“赠给”。

五

那些时辰曾经用轻盈的细工
织就这众目共注的可爱明眸，
终有天对它摆出魔王的面孔，
把绝代佳丽剁成龙钟的老丑：
因为不舍昼夜的时光把盛夏
带到狰狞的冬天去把它结果；
生机被严霜窒息，绿叶又全下，
白雪掩埋了美，满目是赤裸裸：
那时候如果夏天尚未经提炼，
让它凝成香露锁在玻璃瓶里，
美和美的流泽将一起被截断，
美，和美的记忆都无人再提起：
　　但提炼过的花，纵和冬天抗衡，
　　只失掉颜色，却永远吐着清芬。

六

那么，别让冬天嶙峋的手抹掉
你的夏天，在你未经提炼之前：
熏香一些瓶子；把你美的财宝
藏在宝库里，趁它还未及消散。
这样的借贷并不是违禁取利，
既然它使那乐意纳息的高兴；
这是说你该为你另生一个你，
或者，一个生十，就十倍地幸运；
十倍你自己比你现在更快乐，
如果你有十个儿子来重现你：
这样，即使你长辞，死将奈你何，
既然你继续活在你的后裔里？
　　别任性：你那么标致，何必甘心
　　做死的胜利品，让蛆虫做子孙。

七

看，当普照万物的太阳从东方
抬起了火红的头，下界的眼睛
都对他初升的景象表示敬仰，
用目光来恭候他神圣的驾临；
然后他既登上了苍穹的极峰，
像精力饱满的壮年，雄姿英发，
万民的眼睛[①]依旧膜拜他的峥嵘，
紧紧追随着他那疾驰的金驾。
但当他，像耄年拖着尘倦的车轮，
从绝顶颤巍巍地离开了白天，
众目便一齐从他下沉的踪印[②]
移开它们那原来恭顺的视线。
　　同样，你的灿烂的日中一消逝，
　　你就会悄悄死去，如果没后嗣。

---

① 文汇报版为“万民的眼”。
② 踪印　原刊“足印”，据文汇报版修订。

八

我的音乐，为何听音乐会生悲？
甜蜜不相克，快乐使快乐欢笑。
为何爱那你不高兴爱的东西，
或者为何乐于接受你的烦恼？
如果悦耳的声音的完美和谐
和亲挚的协调会惹起你烦忧，
它们不过委婉地责备你不该
用独奏窒息你心中那部合奏。
试看这一根弦，另一根的良人，
怎样融洽地互相呼应和振荡；
宛如父亲、儿子和快活的母亲，
它们联成了一片，齐声在欢唱。
　　它们的无言之歌都异曲同工
　　对你唱着：“你独身就一切皆空。”

九

是否因为怕打湿你寡妇的眼，
你在独身生活里消磨你自己？
哦，如果你不幸无后离开人间，
世界就要哀哭你，像丧偶的妻。
世界将是你寡妇，她永远伤心
你生前没给她留下你的容貌；
其他的寡妇，靠儿女们的眼睛，
反能把良人的肖像在心里长保。
看吧，浪子在世上的种种浪费
只换了主人，世界仍然在享受；
但美的消耗在人间将有终尾：
留着不用，就等于任由它腐朽。
　　这样的心决不会对别人有爱，
　　既然它那么忍心把自己戕害。

一〇

羞呀，否认你并非不爱任何人，
对待你自己却那么欠缺绸缪。
承认，随你便，许多人对你钟情，
但说你并不爱谁，谁也要点头。
因为怨毒的杀机那么缠住你，
你不惜多方设计把自己戕害，
锐意摧残你那座峥嵘的殿宇，
你唯一念头却该是把它重盖。
哦，赶快回心吧，让我也好转意！
难道憎比温婉的爱反得处优？
你那么貌美，愿你也一样心慈，
否则至少对你自己也要温柔。
　　另造一个你吧，你若是真爱我，
　　让美在你儿子或你身上永活。

一一

和你一样快地消沉，你的儿子
也将一样快在世界生长起来；
你灌注给青春的这新鲜血液
仍将是你的，当青春把你抛开。
这里面活着智慧、美丽和昌盛；
没有这，便是愚蠢、衰老和腐朽：
人人都这样想，就要钟停漏尽，
六十年便足使世界化为乌有。
让那些人生来不配生育传宗，
粗鲁、丑陋和笨拙，无后地死去；
造化的至宠，她的馈赠也最丰，
该尽量爱惜她这慷慨的赐予：
　　她把你刻做[①]她的印，意思是要
　　你多印几份，并非要毁掉原稿。

① 即“刻作”。

一二

当我数着壁上报时的自鸣钟，
见明媚的白昼坠入狰狞的夜，
当我凝望着紫罗兰老了春容，
青丝的卷发遍洒着皑皑白雪；
当我看见参天的树枝叶尽脱，
它不久前曾荫蔽喘息的牛羊；
夏天的青翠一束一束地就缚，
带着坚挺的白须被舁上殓床；
于是我不禁为你的朱颜焦虑：
终有天你要加入时光的废堆，
既然美和芳菲都把自己抛弃，
眼看着别人生长自己却枯萎；
　　没什么抵挡得住时光的毒手，
　　除了生育，当他来要把你拘走。

一三

哦，但愿你是你自己，但爱呀，你
终非你有，当你不再活在世上：
对这将临的日子你得要准备，
快交给别人你那俊秀的肖像。
这样，你所租赁的朱颜就永远
不会有满期；于是你又将变成
你自己，当你已经离开了人间，
既然你儿子保留着你的倩影。
谁肯让一座这样的华厦倾颓，
如果小心地看守便可以维护
它的光彩，去抵抗隆冬的狂吹
和那冷酷的死神无情的暴怒？
　　哦，除非是浪子；我爱呀，你知道
　　你有父亲；让你儿子也可自豪。

一四

并非从星辰我采集我的推断；
可是我以为我也精通占星学，
但并非为了推算气运的通蹇，
以及饥荒、瘟疫或四时的风色；
我也不能为短促的时辰算命，
指出每个时辰的雷电和风雨，
或为国王占卜流年是否亨顺，
依据我常从上苍探得的天机。
我的术数只得自你那双明眸，
恒定的双星，它们预兆这吉祥：
只要你回心转意肯储蓄传后，
真和美将双双偕你永世其昌。
　　要不然关于你我将这样昭示：
　　你的末日也就是真和美的死。

一五

当我默察一切活泼泼的生机
保持它们的芳菲都不过一瞬，
宇宙的舞台只搬弄一些把戏
被上苍的星宿在冥冥中牵引；
当我发觉人和草木一样蕃衍，
任同一的天把他鼓励和阻挠，
少壮时欣欣向荣，盛极又必反，
繁华和璀璨都被从记忆抹掉；
于是这一切奄忽浮生的征候
便把妙龄的你在我眼前呈列，
眼见残暴的时光与腐朽同谋，
要把你青春的白昼化作黑夜；
　　为了你的爱我将和时光争持：
　　他摧折你，我要把你重新接枝。

一六

但是为什么不用更凶的法子
去抵抗这血淋淋的魔王——时光？
不用比我的枯笔吉利的武器，
去防御你的衰朽，把自己加强？
你现在站在黄金时辰的绝顶，
许多少女的花园，还未经播种，
贞洁地切盼你那绚烂的群英，
比你的画像更酷肖你的真容：
只有生命的线能把生命重描；
时光的画笔，或者我这支弱管，
无论内心的美或外貌的姣好，
都不能使你在人们眼前活现。
　　献出你自己依然保有你自己，
　　而你得活着，靠你自己的妙笔。

一七

未来的时代谁会相信我的诗，
如果它充满了你最高的美德？
虽然，天知道，它只是一座墓地
埋着你的生命和一半的本色。
如果我写得出你美目的流盼，
用清新的韵律细数你的秀妍，
未来的时代会说："这诗人撒谎：
这样的天姿哪里会落在人间！"
于是我的诗册，被岁月所熏黄，
就要被人藐视，像饶舌的老头；
你的真容被诬作诗人的疯狂，
以及一支古歌的夸张的节奏：
　　但那时你若有个儿子在人世，
　　你就活两次：在他身上，在诗里。

一八

我怎么能够把你来比作夏天？
你不独比它可爱也比它温婉：
狂风把五月宠爱的嫩蕊作践，
夏天出赁的期限又未免太短：
天上的眼睛有时照得太酷烈，
它那炳耀的金颜又常遭掩蔽：
被机缘或无常的天道所摧折，
没有芳艳不终于凋残或消毁。
但是你的长夏永远不会凋落，
也不会损失你这皎洁的红芳，
或死神夸口你在他影里漂泊，
当你在不朽的诗里与时同长。
　　只要一天有人类，或人有眼睛，
　　这诗将长存，并且赐给你生命。

一九

饕餮的时光，去磨钝雄狮的爪，
命大地吞噬自己宠爱的幼婴，
去猛虎的颚下把它利牙拔掉，
焚毁长寿的凤凰，灭绝它的种，
使季节在你飞逝时或悲或喜；
而且，捷足的时光，尽肆意摧残
这大千世界和它易谢的芳菲；
只有这极恶大罪我禁止你犯：
哦，别把岁月刻在我爱的额上，
或用古老的铁笔乱画下皱纹：
在你的飞逝里不要把它弄脏，
好留给后世永作美丽的典型。
　　但，尽管猖狂，老时光，凭你多狠，
　　我的爱在我诗里将万古长青。

二〇

你有副女人的脸，由造化亲手
塑就，你，我热爱的情妇兼情郎；
有颗女人的温婉的心，但没有
反复和变幻，像女人的假心肠；
眼睛比她明媚，又不那么造作，
流盼把一切事物都镀上黄金；
绝世的美色，驾御着一切美色，
既使男人晕眩，又使女人震惊。
开头原是把你当女人来创造：
但造化塑造你时，不觉着了迷，
误加给你一件东西，这就剥掉
我的权利——这东西对我毫无意义。
　　但造化造你既专为女人愉快，
　　让我占有，而她们享受，你的爱。

二一

我的诗神[1]并不像那一位诗神
只知运用脂粉涂抹他的诗句，
连苍穹也要搬下来作妆饰品，
罗列每个佳丽去赞他的佳丽，
用种种浮夸的比喻作成对偶，
把他比太阳、月亮、海陆的瑰宝，
四月的鲜花，和这浩荡的宇宙
蕴藏在它的怀里的一切奇妙。
哦，让我既真心爱，就真心歌唱，
而且，相信我，我的爱可以媲美
任何母亲的儿子，虽然论明亮
比不上挂在天空的金色烛台。
　　谁喜欢空话，让他尽说个不穷；
　　我志不在出售，自用不着祷颂。

① 诗神　即诗人，故下面用男性代词“他”字。——译者原注

二二

这镜子决不能使我相信我老，
只要大好韶华和你还是同年；
但当你脸上出现时光的深槽，
我就盼死神来了结我的天年。
因为那一切妆点着你的美丽
都不过是我内心的表面光彩；
我的心在你胸中跳动，正如你
在我的：那么，我怎会比你先衰？
哦，我的爱呵，请千万自己珍重，
像我珍重自己，乃为你，非为我。
怀抱着你的心，我将那么郑重，
像慈母防护着婴儿遭受病魔。
　　别侥幸独存，如果我的心先碎；
　　你把心交我，并非为把它收回。

二三

仿佛舞台上初次演出的戏子
慌乱中竟忘记了自己的角色，
又像被触犯的野兽满腔怒气，
它那过猛的力量反使它胆怯；
同样，缺乏着冷静，我不觉忘掉
举行爱情的仪节的彬彬盛典，
被我爱情的过度重量所压倒，
在我自己的热爱中一息奄奄。
哦，请让我的诗篇做我的辩士，
替我把缠绵的衷曲默默诉说，
它为爱情申诉，并希求着赏赐，
多于那对你絮絮不休的狡舌：
　　请学会去读缄默的爱的情书，
　　用眼睛来听原属于爱的妙术。

二四

我眼睛扮作画家，把你的肖像
描画在我的心版上，我的肉体
就是那嵌着你的姣颜的镜框，
而画家的无上的法宝是透视。
你要透过画家的巧妙去发见
那珍藏你的奕奕真容的地方；
它长挂在我胸内的画室中间，
你的眼睛却是画室的玻璃窗。
试看眼睛多么会帮眼睛的忙：
我的眼睛画你的像，你的却是
开向我胸中的窗，从那里太阳
喜欢去偷看那藏在里面的你。
　　可是眼睛的艺术终欠这高明：
　　它只能画外表，却不认识内心。

二五

让那些人（他们既有吉星高照）
到处夸说他们的显位和高官，
至于我，命运拒绝我这种荣耀，
只暗中独自赏玩我心里所欢。
王公的宠臣舒展他们的金叶
不过像太阳眷顾下的金盏花，
他们的骄傲在自己身上消灭，
一蹙额便足凋谢他们的荣华。
转战沙场的名将不管多功高，
百战百胜后只要有一次失手，
便从功名册上被人一笔勾销，
毕生的勋劳只落得无声无臭：
　　那么，爱人又被爱，我多么幸福！
　　我既不会迁徙，又不怕被驱逐。

二六

我爱情的至尊，你的美德已经
使我这藩属加强对你的拥戴，
我现在寄给你这诗当作使臣，
去向你述职，并非要向你炫才。
职责那么重，我又才拙少俊语，
难免要显得赤裸裸和你相见，
但望你的妙思，不嫌它太粗鄙，
在你灵魂里把它的赤裸裸遮掩；
因而不管什么星照引我前程，
都对我露出一副和悦的笑容，
把华服加给我这寒伧的爱情，
使我配得上你那缱绻的恩宠。
　　那时我才敢对你夸耀我的爱，
　　否则怕你考验我，总要躲起来。

二七

精疲力竭，我赶快到床上躺下，
去歇息我那整天劳顿的四肢；
但马上我的头脑又整装出发，
以劳我的心，当我身已得休息。
因为我的思想，不辞离乡背井，
虔诚地趱程要到你那里进香，
睁大我这双沉沉欲睡的眼睛，
向着瞎子看得见的黑暗凝望；
不过我的灵魂，凭着它的幻眼，
把你的倩影献给我失明的双眸，
像颗明珠在阴森的夜里高悬，
变老丑的黑夜为明丽的白昼。
　　这样，日里我的腿，夜里我的心，
　　为你、为我自己，都得不着安宁。

二八

那么，我怎么能够喜洋洋归来，
既然得不着片刻身心的安息？
当白天的压逼入夜并不稍衰，
只是夜继日、日又继夜地压逼？
日和夜平时虽事事各不相下，
却互相携手来把我轮流挫折，
一个用跋涉，一个却呶呶怒骂，
说我离开你更远，虽整天跋涉。
为讨好白天，我告它你是光明，
在阴云密布时你将把它映照。
我又这样说去讨黑夜的欢心：
当星星不眨眼，你将为它闪耀。
　　但天天白天尽拖长我的苦痛，
　　夜夜黑夜又使我的忧思转凶。

二九

当我受尽命运和人们的白眼，
暗暗地哀悼自己的身世飘零，
徒用呼吁去干扰聋聩的昊天，
顾盼着身影，诅咒自己的生辰，
愿我和另一个一样富于希望，
面貌相似，又和他一样广交游，
希求这人的渊博，那人的内行，
最赏心的乐事觉得最不对头；
可是，当我正要这样看轻自己，
忽然想起了你，于是我的精神，
便像云雀破晓从阴霾的大地
振翮上升，高唱着圣歌在天门：

　　一想起你的爱使我那么富有，
　　和帝王换位我也不屑于屈就。

三〇

当我传唤对已往事物的记忆
出庭于那馨香的默想的公堂，
我不禁为命中许多缺陷叹息，
带着旧恨，重新哭蹉跎的时光；
于是我可以淹没那枯涸的眼，
为了那些长埋在夜台的亲朋，
哀悼着许多音容俱渺的美艳，
痛哭那情爱久已勾消的哀痛：
于是我为过去的惆怅而惆怅，
并且一一细算，从痛苦到痛苦，
那许多呜咽过的呜咽的旧账，
仿佛还未付过，现在又来偿付。
　　但是只要那刻我想起你，挚友，
　　损失全收回，悲哀也化为乌有。

三一

你的胸怀有了那些心而越可亲
（它们的消逝我只道已经死去）；
原来爱，和爱的一切可爱部分，
和埋掉的友谊都在你怀里藏住。
多少为哀思而流的圣洁泪珠
那虔诚的爱曾从我眼睛偷取
去祭奠死者！我现在才恍然大悟
他们只离开我去住在你的心里。
你是座收藏已往恩情的芳塚，
满挂着死去的情人的纪念牌，
他们把我的馈赠尽向你呈贡，
你独自享受许多人应得的爱。
　　在你身上我瞥见他们的倩影，
　　而你，他们的总和，尽有我的心。

三二

倘你活过我踌躇满志的大限，
当鄙夫“死神”用黄土把我掩埋，
偶然重翻这拙劣可怜的诗卷，
你情人生前写来献给你的爱，
把它和当代俊逸的新诗相比，
发觉它的词笔处处都不如人，
请保留它专为我的爱，而不是
为那被幸运的天才凌驾的韵。
哦，那时候就请赐给我这爱思：
“要是我朋友的诗神与时同长，
他的爱就会带来更美的产儿，
可和这世纪任何杰作同俯仰：
　　但他既死去，诗人们又都迈进，
　　我读他们的文采，却读他的心。”

三三

多少次我曾看见灿烂的朝阳
用他那至尊的眼媚悦着山顶，
金色的脸庞吻着青碧的草场，
把黯淡的溪水镀成一片黄金：
然后蓦地任那最卑贱的云彩
带着黑影驰过他神圣的霁颜，
把他从这凄凉的世界藏起来，
偷移向西方去掩埋他的污点；
同样，我的太阳曾在一个清朝
带着辉煌的光华临照我前额；
但是唉！他只一刻是我的荣耀，
下界的乌云已把他和我遮隔。
　　我的爱却并不因此把他鄙贱，
　　天上的太阳有瑕疵，何况人间！

三四

为什么预告那么璀璨的日子，
哄我不携带大衣便出来游行，
让鄙贱的乌云中途把我侵袭，
用臭腐的烟雾遮蔽你的光明？
你以为现在冲破乌云来晒干
我脸上淋漓的雨点便已满足？
须知无人会赞美这样的药丹：
只能医治创伤，但洗不了耻辱。
你的愧赧也无补于我的心疼；
你虽已忏悔，我依然不免损失：
对于背着耻辱的十字架的人，
冒犯者引咎只是微弱的慰藉。
　　唉，但你的爱所流的泪是明珠，
　　它们的富丽够赎你的罪有余。

三五

别再为你冒犯我的行为痛苦：
玫瑰花有刺，银色的泉有烂泥，
乌云和蚀把太阳和月亮玷污，
可恶的毛虫把香的嫩蕊盘据。
每个人都有错，我就犯了这点：
运用种种比喻来解释你的恶，
弄脏我自己来洗涤你的罪愆，
赦免你那无可赦免的大错过。
因为对你的败行我加以谅解——
你的原告变成了你的辩护士——
我对你起诉，反而把自己出卖：
爱和憎老在我心中互相排挤，
　　以致我不得不变成你的助手
　　去帮你劫夺我，你，温柔的小偷！

三六

让我承认我们俩一定要分离，
尽管我们那分不开的爱是一体：
这样，许多留在我身上的瑕疵，
将不用你分担，由我独自承起。
你我的相爱全出于一片至诚，
尽管不同的生活把我们隔开，
这纵然改变不了爱情的真纯，
却偷掉许多密约佳期的欢快。
我再也不会高声认你做知己，
生怕我可哀的罪过使你含垢，
你也不能再当众把我来赞美，
除非你甘心使你的名字蒙羞。
　　可别这样做；我既然这样爱你，
　　你是我的，我的荣光也属于你。

三七

像一个衰老的父亲高兴去看
活泼的儿子表演青春的伎俩，
同样，我，受了命运的恶毒摧残，
从你的精诚和美德找到力量。
因为，无论美、门第、财富或才华，
或这一切，或其一，或多于这一切，
在你身上登峰造极，我都把
我的爱在你这个宝藏上嫁接。
那么，我并不残废、贫穷、被轻藐，
既然这种种幻影都那么充实，
使我从你的富裕得满足，并倚靠
你的光荣的一部分安然度日。
　　看，生命的至宝，我暗祝你尽有：
　　既有这心愿，我便十倍地无忧。

三八

我的诗神怎么会找不到诗料，
当你还呼吸着，灌注给我的诗
以你自己的温馨题材——那么美妙
绝不是一般俗笔所能够抄袭？
哦，感谢你自己吧，如果我诗中
有值得一读的献给你的目光：
哪里有哑巴，写到你，不善祷颂——
既然是你自己照亮他的想象？
做第十位艺神吧，你要比凡夫
所祈求的古代九位高明得多；
有谁向你呼吁，就让他献出
一些可以传久远的不朽诗歌。
　　我卑微的诗神如可取悦于世，
　　痛苦属于我，所有赞美全归你。

三九

哦，我怎能不越礼地把你歌颂，
当我的最优美部分全属于你？
赞美我自己对我自己有何用？
赞美你岂不等于赞美我自己？
就是为这点我们也得要分手，
使我们的爱名义上各自独处，
以便我可以，在这样分离之后，
把你该独得的赞美全部献出。
别离呵！你会给我多大的痛创，
倘若你辛酸的闲暇不批准我
拿出甜蜜的情思来款待时光，
用甜言把时光和相思蒙混过——
　　如果你不教我怎样化一为二，
　　使我在这里赞美远方的人儿！

四〇

夺掉我的爱，爱呵，请通通夺去；
看看比你已有的能多些什么？
没什么，爱呵，称得上真情实意[1]；
我所爱早属你，纵使不添这个。
那么，你为爱我而接受我所爱，
我不能对你这享受加以责备；
但得受责备，若甘心自我欺绐，
你故意贪尝不愿接受的东西。
我可以原谅你的掠夺，温柔贼，
虽然你把我仅有的通通偷走；
可是，忍受爱情的暗算，爱晓得，
比憎恨的明伤是更大的烦忧。
　　风流的妩媚，连你的恶也妩媚，
　　尽管毒杀我，我们可别相仇视。

① 意　原刊“义”，指文汇报版修订。

四一

你那放荡不羁所犯的风流罪
（当我有时候远远离开你的心）
与你的美貌和青春那么相配，
无论到哪里，诱惑都把你追寻。
你那么温文，谁不想把你夺取？
那么姣好，又怎么不被人围攻？
而当女人追求，凡女人的儿子
谁能坚苦挣扎，不向她怀里送？
唉！但你总不必把我的位儿占，
并斥责你的美丽和青春的迷惑：
它们引你去犯那么大的狂乱，
使你不得不撕毁了两重誓约：
　　她的，因为你的美诱她去就你；
　　你的，因为你的美对我失信义。

四二

你占有她，并非我最大的哀愁，
可是我对她的爱不能说不深；
她占有你，才是我主要的烦忧，
这爱情的损失更能使我伤心。
爱的冒犯者，我这样原谅你们：
你所以爱她，因为晓得我爱她；
也是为我的原故她把我欺瞒，
让我的朋友替我殷勤款待她。
失掉你，我所失是我情人所获，
失掉她，我朋友却找着我所失；
你俩互相找着，而我失掉两个，
两个都为我的原故把我磨折：
　　但这就是快乐：你和我是一体；
　　甜蜜的阿谀！她却只爱我自己。

四三

我眼睛闭得最紧，看得最明亮：
它们整天只看见无味的东西；
而当我入睡，梦中却向你凝望，
幽暗的火焰，暗地里放射幽辉。
你的影子既能教黑影放光明，
对闭上的眼照耀得那么辉煌，
你影子的形会形成怎样的美景，
在清明的白天里用更清明的光！
我的眼睛，我说，会感到多幸运
若能够凝望你在光天化日中，
既然在死夜里你那不完全的影
对酣睡中闭着的眼透出光容！
　　天天都是黑夜一直到看见你，
　　夜夜是白天当好梦把你显示！

四四

假如我这笨拙的体质是思想，
不做美[1]的距离就不能阻止我，
因为我就会从那迢迢的远方，
无论多隔绝，被带到你的寓所。
那么，纵使我的腿站在那离你
最远的天涯，对我有什么妨碍？
空灵的思想无论想到达哪里，
它立刻可以飞越崇山和大海。
但是唉，这思想毒杀我：我并非思想，
能飞越辽远的万里当你去后；
而只是满盛着泥水的钝皮囊，
就只好用悲泣去把时光伺候；
　　这两种重浊的元素毫无所赐
　　除了眼泪，二者的苦恼的标志。

① 不做美　即“不作美”。

四五

其余两种，轻清的风，净化的火，
一个是我的思想，一个是欲望，
都是和你一起，无论我居何所；
它们又在又不在，神速地来往。
因为，当这两种较轻快的元素
带着爱情的温柔使命去见你，
我的生命，本赋有四大，只守住
两个，就不胜其忧郁，奄奄待毙；
直到生命的结合得完全恢复
由于这两个敏捷使者的来归。
它们现正从你那里回来，欣悉
你起居康吉，在向我欣欣[①]告慰。
　　说完了，我乐，可是并不很长久，
　　我打发它们回去，马上又发愁。

① 欣欣　文汇报版译文“殷殷”。

四六

我的眼和我的心在作殊死战，
怎样去把你姣好的容貌分赃；
眼儿要把心和你的形象隔断，
心儿又不甘愿把这权利相让。
心儿声称你在它的深处潜隐，
从没有明眸闯得进它的宝箱；
被告却把这申辩坚决地否认，
说是你的倩影在它里面珍藏。
为解决这悬案就不得不邀请
我心里所有的住户——思想——协商；
它们的共同的判词终于决定
明眸和亲挚的心应得的分量
　　如下：你的仪表属于我的眼睛，
　　而我的心占有你心里的爱情。

四七

现在我的眼和心缔结了同盟，
为的是互相帮忙和互相救济：
当眼儿渴望要一见你的尊容，
或痴情的心快要给叹气窒息，
眼儿就把你的画像大摆筵桌，
邀请心去参加这图画的盛宴；
有时候眼睛又是心的座上客，
去把它缱绻的情思平均分沾：
这样，或靠你的像或我的依恋，
你本人虽远离还是和我在一起；
你不能比我的情思走得更远，
我老跟着它们，它们又跟着你；
　　或者，它们倘睡着，我眼中的像
　　就把心唤醒，使心和眼都舒畅。

四八

我是多么小心，在未上路之前，
为了留以备用，把琐碎的事物
一一锁在箱子里，使得到保险，
不致被一些奸诈的手所亵渎！
但你，比起你来珠宝也成废品，
你，我最亲最好和唯一的牵挂，
无上的慰安（现在是最大的伤心）
却留下来让每个扒手任意拿。
我没有把你锁进任何保险箱，
除了你不在的地方，而我觉得
你在，那就是我的温暖的心房，
从那里你可以随便进进出出；
　　就是在那里我还怕你被偷走：
　　看见这样珍宝，忠诚也变扒手。

四九

为抵抗那一天，要是终有那一天，
当我看见你对我的缺点蹙额，
当你的爱已花完最后一文钱，
被周详的顾虑催去清算账目；
为抵抗那一天，当你像生客走过，
不用那太阳——你眼睛——向我致候，
当爱情，已改变了面目，要搜罗
种种必须决绝的庄重的理由；
为抵抗那一天我就躲在这里，
在对自已的恰当评价内安身，
并且高举我这只手当众宣誓，
为你的种种合法的理由保证：
　　抛弃可怜的我，你有法律保障，
　　既然为什么爱，我无理由可讲。

五〇

多么沉重地我在旅途上跋涉，
当我的目的地（我倦旅的终点）
唆使安逸和休憩这样对我说：
“你又离开了你的朋友那么远！”
那驮我的畜牲，经不起我的忧厄，
驮着我心里的重负慢慢地走，
仿佛这畜牲凭某种本能晓得
它主人不爱快，因为离你远游：
有时恼怒用那血淋淋的靴钉
猛刺它的皮，也不能把它催促；
它只是沉重地报以一声呻吟，
对于我，比刺它的靴钉还要残酷，
　　因为这呻吟使我省悟和熟筹：
　　我的忧愁在前面，快乐在后头。

五一

这样，我的爱就可原谅那笨兽
（当我离开你），不嫌它走得太慢：
从你所在地我何必匆匆跑走？
除非是归来，绝对不用把路赶。
那时可怜的畜牲怎会得宽容，
当极端的迅速还要显得迟钝？
那时我就要猛刺，纵使在御风，
如飞的速度我只觉得是停顿：
那时就没有马能和欲望齐驱；
因此，欲望，由最理想的爱构成，
就引颈长嘶，当它火似的飞驰；
但爱，为了爱，将这样饶恕那畜牲：
　　既然别你的时候它有意慢走，
　　归途我就下来跑，让它得自由。

五二

我像那富翁，他那幸运的钥匙
能把他带到他的心爱的宝藏，
可是他并不愿时常把它启视，
以免磨钝那难得的锐利快感[①]。
所以过节是那么庄严和希有，
因为在一年中仅疏疏地来临，
就像宝石在首饰上稀稀嵌就，
或大颗的珍珠在璎珞上晶莹。
同样，那保存你的时光就好像
我的宝箱，或装着华服的衣橱，
以便偶一重展那被囚的宝光，
使一些幸福的良辰分外幸福。
　　你真运气，你的美德能够使人
　　有你，喜洋洋，你不在，不胜憧憬。

① 锐利快感　原刊“锐利的快感”，据文汇报版修订。

五三

你的本质是什么，用什么造成，
使得万千个倩影都追随着你？
每人都只有一个，每人，一个影；
你一人，却能幻作千万个影子。
试为阿都尼[①]写生，他的画像
不过是模仿你的拙劣的赝品；
尽量把美容术施在海伦[②]颊上，
便是你披上希腊妆的新的真身。
一提起春的明媚和秋的丰饶，
一个把你的绰约的倩影显示，
另一个却是你的慷慨的写照；
一切天生的俊秀都蕴含着你。
　　一切外界的妩媚都有你的份，
　　但谁都没有你那颗坚贞的心。

---

① 阿都尼（Adonis）　又译“阿多尼斯”，古希腊神话中的美男子。
② 海伦（Helen）　古希腊神话中的美女。

五四

哦，美看起来要更美得多少倍，
若再有真加给它温馨的装潢！
玫瑰花很美，但我们觉得它更美，
因为它吐出一缕甜蜜的芳香。
野蔷薇的姿色也是同样旖旎，
比起玫瑰的芳馥四溢的姣颜，
同挂在刺上[①]，同样会搔首弄姿，
当夏天呼息使它的嫩蕊轻展：
但它们唯一的美德只在色相，
开时无人眷恋，萎谢也无人理；
寂寞地死去。香的玫瑰却两样；
它那温馨的死可以酿成香液：
　　你也如此，美丽而可爱的青春，
　　当韶华凋谢，诗提取你的纯精。

① 刺上　原刊“树上”，据文汇报版修订。

五五

没有云石或王公们金的墓碑
能够和我这些强劲的诗比寿；
你将永远闪耀于这些诗篇里，
远胜过那被时光涂脏的石头。
当着残暴的战争把铜像推翻，
或内讧把城池荡成一片废墟，
无论战神的剑或战争的烈焰
都毁不掉你的遗芳的活历史。
突破死亡和湮没一切的仇恨，
你将昂然站起来：对你的赞美
将在万世万代的眼睛里彪炳，
直到这世界消耗完了的末日。
　　这样，直到最后审判把你唤醒，
　　你长在诗里和情人眼里辉映。

五六

温柔的爱，恢复你的劲：别被说
你的刀锋赶不上食欲那样快，
食欲只今天饱餐后暂觉满足，
到明天又照旧一样饕餮起来：
愿你，爱呵，也一样：你那双饿眼
尽管今天已饱看到腻得直眨，
明天还得看，别让长期的瘫痪
把那爱情的精灵活生生窒煞：
让这凄凉的间歇恰像那隔断
两岸的海洋，那里一对新情侣[①]
每天到岸边相会，当他们看见
爱的来归，心里感到加倍欢愉；
　　否则，唤它做[②]冬天，充满了忧悒，
　　使夏至三倍受欢迎，三倍希奇。

---

① 新情侣　原刊无“新”字，据文汇报版补正。
② 唤它做　即“唤它作”。

五七

既然是你奴隶，我有什么可做，
除了时时刻刻伺候你的心愿？
我毫无宝贵的时间可以消磨[①]，
也无事可做，直到你有所驱遣。
我不敢骂那绵绵无尽的时刻，
当我为你，主人，把时辰来看守；
也不敢埋怨别离是多么残酷，
在你已经把你的仆人辞退后；
也不敢用妒忌的念头去探索
你究竟在哪里，或者为什么忙碌，
只是，像个可怜的奴隶，呆想着
你所在的地方，人们会多幸福。
　　爱这呆子是那么无救药的呆
　　凭你为所欲为，他都不觉得坏。

① 可以消磨　原刊“可消磨”，据文汇报版补正。

五八

那使我做你奴隶的神不容我，
如果我要管制你行乐的时光，
或者清算你怎样把日子消磨，
既然是奴隶，就得听从你放浪：
让我忍受，既然什么都得依你，
你那自由的离弃（于我是监牢）；
让忍耐，惯了，接受每一次申斥，
绝不会埋怨你对我损害分毫。
无论你高兴到哪里，你那契约
那么有效，你自有绝对的主权
去支配你的时间；你犯的罪过
你也有主权随意把自己赦免。
　　我只能等待，虽然等待是地狱，
　　不责备你行乐，任它是善或恶。

五九

如果天下无新事，现在的种种
从前都有过，我们的头脑多上当，
当它苦心要创造，却怀孕成功
一个前代有过的婴孩的重担！
哦，但愿历史能用回溯的眼光
（纵使太阳已经运行了五百周），
在古书里对我显示你的肖像，
自从心灵第一次写成了句读！——
让我晓得古人曾经怎样说法，
关于你那雍容的体态的神奇；
是我们高明，还是他们优越，
或者所谓演变其实并无二致。
　　哦，我敢肯定，不少才子在前代
　　曾经赞扬过远不如你的题材。

六〇

像波浪滔滔不息地滚向沙滩：
我们的光阴息息奔赴着终点；
后浪和前浪不断地循环替换，
前推后涌[①]，一个个在奋勇争先。
生辰，一度涌现于光明的金海，
爬行到壮年，然后，既登上极顶，
凶冥的日蚀便遮没它的光彩，
时光又撕毁了它从前的赠品。
时光戳破了青春颊上的光艳，
在美的前额挖下深陷的战壕，
自然的至珍都被它肆意狂啖，
一切挺立的都难逃它的镰刀：
　　可是我的诗未来将屹立千古，
　　歌颂你的美德，不管它多残酷！

① 前推后涌　原刊“前推后拥”，据文汇报版修订。

六一

你是否故意用影子使我垂垂
欲闭的眼睛睁向恹恹[1]的长夜?
你是否要我辗转反侧不成寐,
用你的影子来玩弄我的视野?
那可是从你那里派来的灵魂
远离了家园,来刺探我的行为,
来找我的荒废和耻辱的时辰,
和执行你妒忌[2]的职权和范围?
不呀!你的爱,虽多,并不那么大:
是我的爱使我张开我的眼睛,
是我的真情把我的睡眠打垮,
为你的缘故一夜守候到天明!
　　我为你守夜,而你在别处清醒,
　　远远背着我,和别人却太靠近。

---

① 恹恹　原刊“厌厌”,据文汇报版修订。
② 你妒忌　原刊“你的妒忌”,据文汇报版修订。

六二

自爱这罪恶占据着我的眼睛，
我整个的灵魂和我身体各部；
而对这罪恶什么药石都无灵，
在我心内扎根扎得那么深固。
我相信我自己的眉目最秀丽，
态度最率真，胸怀又那么俊伟；
我的优点对我这样估计自己：
不管哪一方面我都出类拔萃。
但当我的镜子照出我的真相，
全被那焦黑的老年剁得稀烂，
我对于自爱又有相反的感想：
这样溺爱着自己实在是罪愆。
　　我歌颂自己就等于把你歌颂，
　　用你的青春来粉刷我的隆冬。

六三

像我现在一样，我爱人将不免
被时光的毒手所粉碎和消耗，
当时辰吮干他的血，使他的脸
布满了皱纹；当他韶年的清朝
已经爬到暮年的巉岩的黑夜，
使他所占领的一切风流逸韵
都渐渐消灭或已经全部消灭，
偷走了他的春天所有的至珍；
为那时候我现在就厉兵秣马
去抵抗凶暴时光的残酷利刃，
使他无法把我爱的芳菲抹煞，
虽则他能够砍断我爱的生命。
　　他的丰韵将在这些诗里现形，
　　墨迹长在，而他也将万古长青。

六四

当我眼见前代的富丽和豪华
被时光的手毫不留情地磨灭；
当巍峨的塔我眼见沦为碎瓦，
连不朽的铜也不免一场浩劫；
当我眼见那欲壑难填的大海
一步一步把岸上的疆土侵蚀，
汪洋的水又渐渐被陆地覆盖，
失既变成了得，得又变成了失；
当我看见这一切扰攘和废兴，
或者连废兴一旦也化为乌有；
毁灭便教我再三这样地反省：
时光终要跑来把我的爱带走。
　　哦，多么致命的思想！它只能够
　　哭着去把那刻刻怕失去的占有。

六五

既然铜、石，或大地，或无边的海，
没有不屈服于那阴惨的无常，
美，她的活力比一朵花还柔脆，
怎能和他那肃杀的严威抵抗？
哦，夏天温馨的呼息怎能支持
残暴的日子刻刻猛烈的轰炸，
当岩石，无论多么险固，或钢扉，
无论多坚强，都要被时光熔化？
哦，骇人的思想！时光的珍饰，唉，
怎能够不被收进时光的宝箱？
什么劲手能挽他的捷足回来，
或者谁能禁止他把美丽夺抢？
　　哦，没有谁，除非这奇迹有力量：
　　我的爱在翰墨里永久放光芒。

六六

厌了这一切，我向安息的死疾呼，
比方，眼见天才注定做叫化子，
无聊的草包打扮得衣冠楚楚，
纯洁的信义不幸而被人背弃，
金冠可耻地戴在行尸的头上，
处女的贞操遭受暴徒的玷辱，
严肃的正义被人非法地诟让，
壮士被当权的跛子弄成残缺，
愚蠢摆起博士架子驾驭才能，
艺术被官府统治得结舌箝口，
淳朴的真诚被人瞎称为愚笨，
囚徒“善”不得不把统帅“恶”伺候：
　　厌了这一切，我要离开人寰，
　　但，我一死，我的爱人便孤单。

六七

唉，我的爱为什么要和臭腐同居，
把他的绰约的丰姿让人亵渎，
以致[①]罪恶得以和他结成伴侣，
涂上纯洁的外表来眩耀[②]耳目？
骗人的脂粉为什么要替他写真，
从他的奕奕神采偷取死形似？
为什么，既然他是玫瑰花的真身，
可怜的美还要找玫瑰的影子？
为什么他得活着，当造化破了产，
缺乏鲜血去灌注淡红的脉络？
因为造化现在只有他作富源，
自夸富有，却靠他的利润过活。
　　哦，她珍藏他，为使荒歉的今天
　　认识从前曾有过怎样的丰年。

---

① 以致 原刊“以至”，据文汇报版修订。
② 眩耀 即“炫耀”。

六八

这样，他的朱颜是古代的图志，
那时美开了又谢像今天花一样，
那时冒牌的艳色还未曾出世，
或未敢公然高据活人的额上，
那时死者的美发，坟墓的财产，
还未被偷剪下来，去活第二回
在第二个头上[①]；那时美的死金鬟
还未被用来使别人显得华贵：
这圣洁的古代在他身上呈现，
赤裸裸的真容，毫无一点铅华，
不用别人的青翠做他的夏天，
不掠取旧脂粉妆饰他的鲜花；
　　就这样造化把他当图志珍藏，
　　让假艺术赏识古代美的真相。

① 在第二个头上　当时制造假发的人常常买死人的头发作原料。——译者原注

六九

你那众目共睹的无瑕的芳容，
谁的心思都不能再加以增改；
众口，灵魂的声音，都一致赞同：
赤的真理，连仇人也无法掩盖。
这样，表面的赞扬载满你仪表；
但同一声音，既致应有的崇敬，
便另换口吻去把这赞扬勾消，
当心灵看到眼看不到的内心。
它们向你那灵魂的美的海洋
用你的操行作测量器去探究，
于是吝啬的思想，眼睛虽大方，
便加给你的鲜花以野草的恶臭：
　　为什么你的香味赶不上外观？
　　土壤是这样，你自然长得平凡。

七〇

你受人指摘，并不是你的瑕疵，
因为美丽永远是诽谤的对象；
美丽的无上的装饰就是猜疑，
像乌鸦在最晴朗的天空飞翔。
所以，检点些，谗言只能更恭维
你的美德，既然时光对你钟情；
因为恶蛆最爱那甜蜜的嫩蕊，
而你的正是纯洁无瑕的初春。
你已经越过年轻日子的埋伏，
或未遭遇袭击，或已克服敌手；
可是，对你这样的赞美并不足
堵住那不断扩大的嫉妒的口：
　　若没有猜疑把你的清光遮掩，
　　多少[①]心灵的王国将归你独占。

---

① 多少　原刊“多少个”，据文汇报版修订。

七一

我死去的时候别再为我悲哀，
当你听见那沉重凄惨的葬钟
普告给全世界说我已经离开
这龌龊世界去伴最龌龊的虫：
不呀，当你读到这诗，别再记起
那写它的手；因为我爱到这样，
宁愿被遗忘在你甜蜜的心里，
如果想起我会使你不胜哀伤。
如果呀，我说，如果你看见这诗，
那时候或许我已经化作泥土，
连我这可怜的名字也别提起，
但愿你的爱与我的生命同腐。
　　免得这聪明世界猜透你的心，
　　在我死去后把你也当作笑柄。

七二

哦，免得这世界要强逼你自招
我有什么好处，使你在我死后
依旧爱我，爱人呀，把我全忘掉，
因为我一点值得提的都没有；
除非你捏造出一些美丽的谎，
过分为我吹嘘我应有的价值，
把瞑目长眠的我阿谀和夸奖，
远超过鄙吝的事实所愿昭示：
哦，怕你的真爱因此显得虚伪，
怕你为爱的原故替我说假话，
愿我的名字永远和肉体同埋，
免得活下去把你和我都羞煞。
　　因为我可怜的作品使我羞惭，
　　而你爱不值得爱的，也该愧赧。

七三

在我身上你或许会看见秋天，
当黄叶，或尽脱，或只三三两两
挂在瑟缩的枯枝上索索抖颤——
荒废的歌坛，那里百鸟曾合唱。
在我身上你或许会看见暮霭，
它在日落后向西方徐徐消退：
黑夜，死的化身，渐渐把它赶开，
严静的安息笼住纷纭的万类。
在我身上你或许会看见余烬，
它在青春的寒灰里奄奄一息，
在惨淡灵床上早晚总要断魂，
给那滋养过它的烈焰所销毁。
　　看见了这些，你的爱就会加强，
　　因为他转瞬要辞你溘然长往。

七四

但是放心吧：当那无情的拘票
终于丝毫不宽假地把我带走，
我的生命在诗里将依然长保，
永生的纪念品，永久和你相守。
当你重读这些诗，就等于重读
我献给你的至纯无二的生命：
尘土只能有它的份，那就是尘土；
灵魂却属你，这才是我的真身。
所以你不过失掉生命的糟粕
（当我肉体死后），恶蛆们的食饵，
无赖的刀下一个怯懦的俘获，
太卑贱的秽物，不配被你记忆。
　　它唯一的价值就在它的内蕴，
　　那就是这诗：这诗将和它长存。

七五

我的心需要你，像生命需要食粮，
或者像大地需要及时的甘霖；
为你的安宁我内心那么凄惶
就像贪夫和他的财富作斗争：
他，有时自夸财主，然后又顾虑
这惯窃的时代会偷他的财宝；
我，有时觉得最好独自伴着你，
忽然又觉得该把你当众夸耀：
有时饱餐秀色后腻到化不开，
渐渐地又饿得慌要瞟你一眼；
既不占有也不追求别的欢快，
除掉那你已施或要施的恩典。

　　这样，我整天垂涎或整天不消化，
　　我狼吞虎咽，或一点也咽不下。

七六

为什么我的诗那么缺新光彩，
赶不上现代善变多姿的风尚？
为什么我不学时人旁征博采
那竞奇斗艳，穷妍极巧的新腔？
为什么我写的始终别无二致，
寓情思旨趣于一些老调陈言，
几乎每一句都说出我的名字，
透露它们的身世，它们的来源？
哦，须知道，我爱呵，我只把你描，
你和爱情就是我唯一的主题；
推陈出新是我的无上的诀窍，
我把开支过的，不断重新开支：
　　因为，正如太阳天天新天天旧，
　　我的爱把说过的事絮絮不休。

七七

镜子将告诉你朱颜怎样消逝，
日规怎样一秒秒耗去你的华年；
这白纸所要记录的你的心迹
将教你细细玩味下面的教言。
你的镜子所忠实反映的皱纹
将令你记起那张开口的坟墓；
从日规上阴影的潜移你将认清
时光走向永劫的悄悄的脚步。
看，把记忆所不能保留的东西
交给这张白纸，在那里面你将
看见你精神的产儿受到抚育，
使你重新认识你心灵的本相。
　　这些日课，只要你常拿来重温，
　　将有利于你，并丰富你的书本。

七八

我常常把你当诗神向你祷告，
在诗里找到那么有力的神助，
以致凡陌生的笔都把我仿效，
在你名义下把他们的诗散布。
你的眼睛，曾教会哑巴们歌唱，
曾教会沉重的愚昧高飞上天，
又把新羽毛加给博学的翅膀，
加给温文尔雅以两重的尊严。
可是我的诗应该最使你骄傲，
它们的诞生全在你的感召下：
对别人的作品你只润饰格调，
用你的美在他们才华上添花。
　　但对于我，你就是我全部艺术，
　　把我的愚拙提到博学的高度。

七九

当初我独自一个恳求你协助，
只有我的诗占有你一切妩媚；
但现在我清新的韵律既陈腐，
我的病诗神只好给别人让位。
我承认，爱呵，你这美妙的题材
值得更高明的笔的精写细描；
可是你的诗人不过向你还债，
他把夺自你的当作他的创造。
他赐你美德，美德这词他只从
你的行为偷取；他加给你秀妍，
其实从你颊上得来；他的歌颂
没有一句不是从你身上发见。
　　那么，请别感激他对你的称赞，
　　既然他只把欠你的向你偿还。

八〇

哦，我写到你的时候多么气馁，
得知有更大天才[①]利用你名字，
他不惜费尽力气去把你赞美，
使我箝口结舌，一提起你声誉！
但你的价值，像海洋一样无边，
不管轻舟或艨艟同样能载起，
我这莽撞的艇，尽管小得可怜，
也向你茫茫的海心大胆行驶。
你最浅的滩濑已足使我浮泛，
而他岸岸然驶向你万顷汪洋；
或者，万一覆没[②]，我只是片轻帆，
他却是结构雄伟，气宇轩昂：
　　如果他安全到达，而我遭失败，
　　最不幸的是：毁我的是我的爱。

---

① 更大天才　原刊“更大的天才”，据文汇报版修订。
① 覆没　原刊“复没”，据文汇报版修订。

八一

无论我将活着为你写墓志铭，
或你未亡而我已在地下腐朽，
纵使我已被遗忘得一干二净，
死神将不能把你的忆念夺走。
你的名字将从这诗里得永生，
虽然我，一去，对人间便等于死；
大地只能够给我一座乱葬坟，
而你却将长埋在人们眼睛里。
我这些小诗便是你的纪念碑，
未来的眼睛固然要百读不厌，
未来的舌头也将要传诵不衰，
当现在呼吸的人已瞑目长眠。
　　这强劲的笔将使你活在生气
　　最蓬勃的地方，在人们的嘴里。

八二

我承认你并没有和我的诗神
结同心，因而可以丝毫无愧地[①]
去俯览那些把你作主题的诗人
对你的赞美，褒奖着每本诗集。
你的智慧和姿色都一样出众，
又发觉你的价值比我的赞美高，
因而你不得不到别处去追踪
这迈进时代的更生动的写照。
就这么办，爱呵，但当他们既已
使尽了浮夸的辞藻把你刻划，
真美的你只能由真诚的知己
用真朴的话把你真实地表达；
　　他们的浓脂粉只配拿去染红
　　贫血的脸颊；对于你却是滥用。

---

① 无愧地　原版“无愧恧”，据文汇报版修订。

八三

我从不觉得你需要涂脂荡粉，
因而从不用脂粉涂你的朱颜；
我发觉，或以为发觉，你的丰韵
远超过诗人献你的无味缱绻：
因此，关于你我的歌只装打盹，
好让你自己生动地现身说法，
证明时下的文笔是多么粗笨，
想把美德，你身上的美德增华。
你把我这沉默认为我的罪行，
其实却应该是我最大的荣光；
因为我不作声，于美丝毫无损，
别人想给你生命，[1]反把你埋葬。
　　你的两位诗人所模拟的赞美，
　　远不如你一只慧眼藏[2]的光辉。

① 此处原刊无标点逗号，据文汇报版修订。
② 慧眼藏　原刊“慧眼所藏”，据文汇报版修订。

八四

谁说得最好？哪个说得更圆满
比起这丰美的赞词：“只有你是你”？
这赞词蕴藏着你的全部资产，
谁和你争妍，就必须和它比拟。
那枝文笔实在是贫瘠得可怜，
如果它不能把题材稍事增华；
但谁写到你，只要他能够表现
你就是你，他的故事已够伟大。
让他只照你原稿忠实地直抄，
别把造化的清新的素描弄坏，
这样的摹本已显出他的巧妙，
使他的风格到处受人们崇拜。
　　你将对你美的祝福加以咒诅：
　　太爱人赞美，连美也变成庸俗。

八五

我的缄口的诗神只脉脉无语；
他们对你的美评却累牍连篇，
用金笔刻成辉煌夺目的大字，
和经过一切艺神雕琢的名言。
我满腔热情，他们却善颂善祷；
像不识字的牧师只知喊“阿门”，
去响应才子们用精炼的笔调
熔铸成的每一首赞美的歌咏。
听见人赞美你，我说，“的确，很对”，
凭他们怎样歌颂我总嫌不够；
但只在心里说，因为我对你的爱
虽拙于词令，行动却永远带头。
　　那么，请敬他们，为他们的虚文；
　　敬我，为我的哑口无言的真诚。

八六

是否他那雄浑的诗句，昂昂然
扬帆直驶去夺取太宝贵的你，
使我成熟的思想在脑里流产，
把孕育它们的胎盘变成墓地？
是否他的心灵，从幽灵学会写
超凡的警句，把我活生生殛毙？
不，既不是他本人，也不是黑夜
他那些助手，能使我的诗昏迷。[①]
他，或他那个和善可亲的幽灵
（它夜夜用机智骗他），都不能自豪
是他们把我打垮，使我默不作声；
他们的威胁绝不能把我吓倒。
　　但当他的诗充满了你的鼓励，
　　我就要缺灵感；这才使我丧气。

① 本句据文汇报版。原刊“遣送给他的助手，能使我昏迷”。

八七

再会吧！你太宝贵[①]，我无法高攀；
显然你也晓得你自己的声价：
你的价值的证券够把你赎还，
我对你的债权只好全部作罢。
因为，不经你批准，怎能[②]占有你？
我哪有福气消受这样的珍宝？
这美惠对于我既然毫无根据，
便不得不取消我的专利执照。
你曾许了我，因为低估了自己，
不然就错识了我，你的受赐者；
因此，你这份厚礼，既出自误会，
就归还给你，经过更好的判决。
　　这样，我曾占有你，像一个美梦，
　　在梦里称王，醒来只是一场空。

---

① 宝贵　原刊“宝贵了”，据文汇报版修订。
② 怎能　原刊“我怎能”，据文汇报版修订。

八八

当你有一天下决心瞧我不起，
用侮蔑的眼光衡量我的轻重，
我将站在你那边打击我自己，
证明你贤德，尽管你已经背盟。
对自己的弱点我既那么内行，
我将为你的利益捏造我种种
无人觉察的过失，把自己中伤；
使你抛弃了我反而得到光荣：
而我也可以借此而大有收获；
因为我全部情思那么倾向你，
我为自己所招惹的一切侮辱
既对你有利，对我就加倍有利。
　　我那么衷心属你，我爱到那样，
　　为你的美誉愿承当一切诽谤。

八九

说你抛弃我是为了我的过失，
我立刻会对这冒犯加以阐说：
叫我做瘸子，我马上两脚都躄，
对你的理由绝不作任何反驳。
为了替你的反复无常找借口，
爱呵，凭你怎样侮辱我，总比不上
我侮辱自己来得厉害；既看透
你心肠，我就要绞杀交情，假装
路人避开你；你那可爱的名字，
那么香，将永不挂在我的舌头，
生怕我，太亵渎了，会把它委屈；
万一还会把我们的旧欢泄漏。
　　我为你将展尽辩才反对自己，
　　因为你所憎恶的，我绝不爱惜。

九〇

恨我，倘你[①]高兴；请现在就开首；
现在，当举世都起来和我作对，
请趁势为命运助威，逼我低头，
别意外地走来作事后的摧毁。
唉，不要，当我的心已摆脱烦恼，
来为一个已克服的厄难作殿，
不要在暴风后再来一个雨朝，
把那注定的浩劫的来临拖延。
如果你要离开我，别等到最后，
当其他的烦忧已经肆尽暴虐；
请一开头就来：让我好先尝够
命运的权威应有尽有的凶恶。
　　于是别的苦痛，现在显得苦痛，
　　比起丧失你来便要无影无踪。

① 倘你　原刊“倘若你”，据文汇报版修订。

九一

有人夸耀门第，有人夸耀技巧，
有人夸耀财富，有人夸耀体力；
有人夸耀新妆，丑怪尽管时髦；
有人夸耀鹰犬，有人夸耀骏骥；
每种嗜好都各饶特殊的趣味，
每一种都各自以为其乐无穷：
可是这些癖好都不合我口味[1]——
我把它们融入更大的乐趣中。
你的爱对我比门第还要豪华，
比财富还要丰裕，比艳妆光彩，
它的乐趣远胜过鹰犬和骏马；
有了你，我便可以笑傲全世界：
　　只有这点可怜：你随时可罢免
　　我这一切，使我成无比的可怜。

① 口味　原刊“口胃”，据文汇报版修订。

九二

但尽管你不顾一切偷偷溜走，
直到生命终点你还是属于我。
生命也不会比你的爱更长久，
因为生命只靠你的爱才能活。
因此，我就不用怕最大的灾害，
既然最小的已足置我于死地。
我瞥见一个对我更幸福的境界，
它不会随着你的爱憎而转移：
你的反复再也不能使我颓丧，
既然你一反脸我生命便完毕。
哦，我找到了多么幸福的保障：
幸福地享受你的爱，幸福地死去！
　　但人间哪有不怕玷污的美满？
　　你可以变心肠，同时对我隐瞒。

九三

于是我将活下去，认定你忠贞，
像被骗的丈夫；于是爱的面目
对我仍旧是爱，虽则已翻了新；
眼睛尽望着我，心儿却在别处：
憎恨既无法存在于你的眼里，
我就无法看出你心肠的改变。
许多人每段假情假义的历史
都在颦眉、蹙额或气色上表现；
但上天造你的时候早已注定
柔情要永远在你的脸上逗留；
不管你的心怎样变幻无凭准，
你眼睛只能诉说旖旎和温柔。
　　你的妩媚会变成夏娃的苹果，
　　如果你的美德跟外表不配合。

九四

谁有力量损害人而不这样干，
谁不做人以为他们爱做的事，
谁使人动情，自己却石头一般，
冰冷、无动于衷，对诱惑能抗拒——
谁就恰当地承受上天的恩宠，
善于贮藏和保管造化的财富；
他们才是自己美貌的主人翁，
而别人只是自己姿色的家奴。
夏天的花把夏天熏得多芳馥，
虽然对自己它只自开又自落，
但是那花若染上卑劣的病毒，
最贱的野草也比它高贵得多：
　　极香的东西一腐烂就成极臭，
　　烂百合花比野草更臭得难受。

九五

耻辱被你弄成多温柔多可爱！
恰像馥郁的玫瑰花心的毛虫，
它把你含苞欲放的美名污败！
哦，多少温馨把你的罪过遮蒙！
那讲述你的生平故事的长舌，
想对你的娱乐作淫猥的评论，
只能用一种赞美口气来贬责：
一提起你名字，诬蔑也变谄佞。
哦，那些罪过找到了多大的华厦，
当它们把你挑选来作安乐窝，
在那儿美为污点披上了轻纱，
在那儿触目的一切都变清和！
　　警惕呵，心肝，为你这特权警惕；
　　最快的刀被滥用也失去锋利！

九六

有人说你的缺点在年少放荡；
有人说你的魅力在年少风流；
魅力和缺点都多少受人赞赏：
缺点变成添在魅力上的锦绣。
宝座上的女王手上戴的戒指，
就是最贱的宝石也受人尊重，
同样，那在你身上出现的瑕疵
也变成真理，当作真理被推崇。
多少绵羊会受到野狼的引诱，
假如野狼戴上了绵羊的面目！
多少爱慕你的人会被你拐走，
假如你肯把你全部力量使出！
　　可别这样做；我既然这样爱你，
　　你是我的，我的荣光[①]也属于你。

---

① 荣光　原刊“光荣”，据文汇报版修订。诗末两行同第36首。

九七

我离开[1]了你，日子多么像严冬，
你，飞逝的流年中唯一的欢乐！
天色多阴暗！我又受尽了寒冻！
触目是龙钟腊月的一片萧索！
可是别离的时期恰好是夏日；
和膨胀着累累的丰收的秋天，
满载着青春的淫荡结下的果实，
好像怀胎的新寡妇，大腹便便：
但是这累累的丰收，在我看来，
只能成无父孤儿和乖异的果；
因夏天和它的欢娱把你款待，
你不在，连小鸟也停止了唱歌；
　　或者，即使它们唱，声调那么沉，
　　树叶全变灰了，生怕冬天降临。

① 我离开　原刊“离开”，据文汇报版修订。

九八

我离开你的时候正好是春天，
当绚烂的四月，披上新的锦袄，
把活泼的春心给万物灌注遍，
连沉重的土星[①]也跟着笑和跳。
可是无论小鸟的歌唱，或万紫
千红、芬芳四溢的一簇簇鲜花，
都不能使我诉说夏天的故事，
或从烂熳的山洼把它们采掐：
我也不羡慕那百合花的洁白，
也不赞美玫瑰花的一片红晕；
它们不过是香，是悦目的雕刻，
你才是它们所要摹拟的真身。
　　因此，于我还是严冬，而你不在，
　　像逗着你影子，我逗它们开怀。

① 土星　土星在西欧星相学里是沉闷和忧郁的象征。——译者原注

九九[1]

我对孟浪的紫罗兰这样谴责：
“温柔贼，你哪里偷来这缕温馨，
若不是从我爱的呼息？这紫色
在你的柔颊上抹了一层红晕，
还不是从我爱的血管里染得？”
我申斥百合花盗用了你的手，
茉沃兰[2]的蓓蕾偷取你的柔发；
站在刺上的玫瑰花吓得直抖，
一朵羞得通红，一朵绝望到发白，
另一朵，不红不白，从双方偷来；
还在赃物上添上了你的呼息，
但，[3]既犯了盗窃，当它正昂头盛开，
一条怒冲冲的毛虫把它咬死。
　　我还看见许多花，但没有一朵
　　不从你那里偷取芬芳和婀娜。

---

① 这首多了一行。——译者原注
② 茉沃兰（marjoram），又译“墨角兰”“马郁兰”。
③ 此处原刊缺逗号，据文汇报版修订。

一〇〇

你在哪里，诗神，竟长期忘记掉
把你的一切力量的源头歌唱？
为什么浪费狂热于一些滥调，
消耗你的光去把俗物照亮？
回来吧，健忘的诗神，立刻轻弹
宛转的旋律，赎回虚度的光阴；
唱给那衷心爱慕你并把灵感
和技巧赐给你的笔的耳朵听。
起来，懒诗神，检查我爱的秀容，
看时光可曾在那里刻下皱纹；
假如有，就要尽量把衰老嘲讽，
使时光的剽窃到处遭人齿冷。
　　快使爱成名，趁时光未下手前，
　　你就挡得住它的风刀和霜剑。

一〇一

偷懒的诗神呵，你将怎样补救
你对那被美渲染的真的怠慢？
真和美都与我的爱相依相守；
你也一样，要倚靠它才得通显。
说吧，诗神；你或许会这样回答：
“真的固定色彩不必用色彩绘；
美也不用翰墨把美的真容画；
用不着搀杂，完美永远是完美。”
难道他不需要赞美，你就不作声？
别替缄默辩护，因为你有力量
使他比镀金的坟墓更享遐龄，
并在未来的年代永受人赞扬。
　　当仁不让吧，诗神，我要教你怎样
　　使他今后和现在一样受景仰。

一〇二

我的爱加强了，虽然看来更弱；
我的爱一样热，虽然表面稍冷：
谁把他心中的崇拜到处传播，
就等于把他的爱情看作商品。
我们那时才新恋，又正当春天，
我惯用我的歌去欢迎它来归，
像夜莺在夏天门前彻夜清啭，
到了盛夏的日子便停止歌吹。
并非现在夏天没有那么惬意
比起万籁静听它哀唱的时候，
只为狂欢的音乐载满每一枝，
太普通，意味便没有那么深悠。
　　所以，像它，我有时也默默无言，
　　免得我的歌，太繁了，使你烦厌。

一〇三

我的诗神的产品多贫乏可怜！
分明有无限天地可炫耀才华，
可是她的题材，尽管一无妆点，
比加上我的赞美价值还要大！
别非难我，如果我写不出什么！
照照镜子吧，看你镜中的面孔
多么超越我的怪笨拙的创作，
使我的诗失色，叫我无地自容。
那可不是罪过吗，努力要增饰，
反而把原来无瑕的题材涂毁？
因为我的诗并没有其他目的，
除了要模仿你的才情和妩媚；
　　是的，你的镜子，当你向它端详，
　　所反映的远远多于我的诗章。

一〇四

对于我，俊友，你永远不会衰老，
因为自从我的眼碰见你的眼，
你还是一样美。三个严冬摇掉
三个苍翠的夏天的树叶和光艳，
三个阳春三度化作秋天的枯黄。
时序使我三度看见四月的芳菲
三度被六月的炎炎烈火烧光。
但你，还是和初见时一样明媚；
唉，可是美，像时针，它蹑着脚步
移过钟面，你看不见它的踪影；
同样，你的姣颜，我以为是常驻，
其实在移动，迷惑的是我的眼睛。
　　颤栗吧，未来的时代，听我呼吁：
　　你还没有生，美的夏天已死去。

一〇五

不要把我的爱叫作偶像崇拜，
也不要把我的爱人当偶像看，
既然所有我的歌和我的赞美
都献给一个，为一个，永无变换。
我的爱今天仁慈，明天也仁慈，
有着惊人的美德，永远不变心，
所以我的诗也一样坚贞不渝，
全省掉差异，只叙述一件事情。
“美、善和真”，就是我全部的题材，
“美、善和真”，用不同的词句表现；
我的创造就在这变化上演才，
三题一体，它的境界可真无限。
　　过去“美、善和真”常常分道扬镳，
　　到今天才在一个人身上协调。

一〇六

当我从那湮远的古代的纪年
发见那绝代风流人物的写真，
艳色使得古老的歌咏也香艳，
颂赞着多情骑士和绝命佳人，
于是，从那些国色天姿的描画，
无论手脚、嘴唇，或眼睛或眉额，
我发觉那些古拙的笔所表达
恰好是你现在所占领的姿色。
所以他们的赞美无非是预言
我们这时代，一切都预告着你；
不过他们观察只用想象的眼，
还不够才华把你歌颂得尽致：
　　而我们，幸而得亲眼看见今天，
　　只有眼惊羡，却没有舌头咏叹。

一〇七

无论我自己的忧虑，或那梦想着
未来的这茫茫世界的先知灵魂，
都不能限制我的真爱的租约，
纵使它已注定作命运的抵偿品。
人间的月亮已度过被蚀的灾难，
不祥的占卜把自己的预言嘲讽，
动荡和疑虑既已获得了保险，
和平在宣告橄榄枝永久葱茏。
于是在这时代甘露的遍洒下，
我的爱面貌一新，而死神降伏，
既然我将活在这拙作里，任凭他
把那些愚钝的无言的种族凌辱。
　　你将在这里找着你的纪念碑，
　　魔王的金盔和铜墓却被销毁。

一〇八

脑袋里有什么，笔墨形容得出，
我这颗真心不已经对你描画？
还有什么新东西可说可记录，
以表白我的爱或者你的真价？
没有，乖乖；可是，像虔诚[①]的祷词
我没有一天不把它复说一遍；
老话并不老；你属我，我也属你，
就像我祝福你名字的头一天。
所以永恒的爱在常青[②]爱匣里
不会蒙受年岁的损害和尘土，
不会让皱纹占据应有的位置，
反而把老时光当作永久的家奴；
　　发觉最初的爱苗依旧得保养，
　　尽管时光和外貌都盼它枯黄。

① 像虔诚　原刊无“像”字，据文汇报版补正。
② 常青　原刊“长青”，据文汇报版修订。

一〇九

哦，千万别埋怨我改变过心肠，
别离虽似乎减低了我的热情。
正如我抛不开自己远走他方，
我也一刻离不开你，我的灵魂。
你是我的爱的家：我虽曾流浪，
现在已经像远行的游子归来；
并准时到家，没有跟时光改样，
而且把洗涤我污点的水带来。
哦，请千万别相信（尽管我难免
和别人一样经不起各种试诱）
我的天性会那么荒唐和鄙贱
竟抛弃你这至宝去追求乌有；
　　这无垠的宇宙对我都是虚幻；
　　你才是，我的玫瑰，我全部财产。

一一〇

唉，我的确曾经常东奔西跑，
扮作斑衣的小丑供众人赏玩，
违背我的意志，把至宝贱卖掉，
为了新交不惜把旧知交冒犯；
更千真万确我曾经斜着冷眼
去看真情；但天呀，这种种离乖
给我的心带来了另一个春天，
最坏的考验证实了你的真爱。
现在一切都过去了，请你接受
无尽的友谊：我不再把欲望磨利，
用新的试探去考验我的老友——
那拘禁我的、钟情于我的神祇。
　　那么，欢迎我吧，我的人间的天，
　　迎接我到你最亲的纯洁的胸间。

一一一

哦，请为我把命运的女神诟让，
她是嗾使[①]我造成业障的主犯，
因为她对我的生活别无赡养，
除了养成我粗鄙的众人米饭。
因而我的名字就把烙印[②]接受，
也几乎为了这缘故我的天性
被职业所玷污，如同染工的手：
可怜我吧，并祝福我获得更新；
像个温顺的病人，我甘心饮服
涩嘴的醋[③]来消除我的重感染；
不管它多苦，我将一点不觉苦，
也不辞两重忏悔以赎我的罪愆。
　　请怜悯我吧，挚友，我向你担保
　　你的怜悯已经够把我医治好。

① 嗾使　即“唆使”。
② 烙印　耻辱。——译者原注
③ 涩嘴的醋　当时相信醋能防疫。——译者原注

一一二

你的爱怜抹掉那世俗的讥谗
打在我的额上的耻辱的烙印；
别人的毁誉对我有什么相干，
你既表扬我的善又把恶遮隐！
你是我整个宇宙，我必须努力
从你的口里听取我的荣和辱；
我把别人，别人把我，都当作死，
谁能使我的铁心肠变善或变恶？
别人的意见我全扔入了深渊，
那么干净，我简直像聋蛇一般，
凭他奉承或诽谤都充耳不闻。
请倾听我怎样原谅我的冷淡：
　　你那么根深蒂固长在我心里，
　　全世界，除了你，我都认为死去。

一一三

自从离开你，眼睛便移居心里，
于是那双指挥我行动的眼睛，
既把职守分开，就成了半瞎子，
自以为还看见，其实已经失明；
因为它们所接触的任何形状，
花鸟或姿态，都不能再传给心，
自己也留不住把捉到的景象；
一切过眼的事物心儿都无份。
因为一见粗俗或幽雅的景色，
最畸形的怪物或绝艳的面孔，
山或海，日或夜，乌鸦或者白鸽，
眼睛立刻塑成你美妙的姿容。
　　心中满是你，什么再也装不下，
　　就这样我的真心教眼睛说假话。

一一四

是否我的心，既把你当王冠戴，
喝过帝王们的鸩毒——自我阿谀？
还是我该说，我眼睛说的全对，
因为你的爱教会它这炼金术，
使它能够把一切蛇神和牛鬼
转化为和你一样柔媚的天婴，
把每个丑恶改造成尽善尽美，
只要事物在它的柔辉下现形？
哦，是前者；是眼睛的自我陶醉，
我伟大的心灵把它一口喝尽：
眼睛晓得投合我心灵的口味，
为它准备好这杯可口的毒饮。
　　尽管杯中有毒，罪过总比较轻，
　　因为先爱上它的是我的眼睛。

一一五

我从前写的那些诗全都撒谎，
连那些说“我爱你到极点”在内，
可是那时候我的确无法想象
白热的火还发得出更大光辉。
只害怕时光的无数意外事故
钻进密约间，勾销帝王的意旨，
晒黑美色，并挫钝锋锐的企图，
使倔强的心屈从事物的隆替：
唉，为什么，既怵于时光的专横，
我不可说，“现在我爱你到极点”，[1]
当我摆脱掉疑虑，充满着信心，
觉得来日不可期，只掌握目前？
　　爱是婴儿；难道我不可这样讲，
　　去促使在生长中的羽毛丰满？

① 本行末标点据文汇报版。

一一六

我绝不承认两颗真心的结合
会有任何障碍；爱算不得真爱，
若是一看见人家改变便转舵，
或者一看见人家转弯便离开。
哦，决不！爱是亘古长明的塔灯，
它定睛望着风暴却兀不为动；
爱又是指引迷舟的一颗恒星，
你可量它多高，它所值却无穷。
爱不受时光的播弄，尽管红颜
和皓齿难免遭受时光的毒手；
爱并不因瞬息的改变而改变，
它巍然矗立直到末日的尽头。
　　我这话若说错，并被证明不确，
　　就算我没写诗，也没人真爱过。

一一七

请这样控告我：说我默不作声，
尽管对你的深恩我应当酬谢；
说我忘记向你缱绻的爱慰问，
尽管我对你依恋一天天密切；
说我时常和陌生的心灵来往，
为偶尔机缘断送你宝贵情谊；
说我不管什么风都把帆高扬，
任它们把我吹到天涯海角去。
请把我的任性和错误都记下，
在真凭实据上还要积累嫌疑，
把我带到你的颦眉蹙额底下，
千万别唤醒怨毒来把我射死；
　　因为我的诉状说我急于证明
　　你对我的爱多么忠贞和坚定。

一一八

好比我们为了促使食欲增进，
用种种辛辣调味品刺激胃口；
又好比服清泻剂以预防大病，
用较轻的病截断重症的根由；
同样，饱尝了你的不腻人的甜蜜，
我选上苦酱来当作我的食料；
厌倦了健康，觉得病也有意思，
尽管我还没有到生病的必要。
这样，为采用先发制病的手段，
爱的策略变成了真实的过失：
我对健康的身体乱投下药丹，
用痛苦来把过度的幸福疗治。
　　但我由此取得这真正的教训：
　　药也会变毒，谁若因爱你而生病。

一一九

我曾喝下了多少鲛人的泪珠
从我心中地狱般的锅里蒸出来，
把恐惧当希望，又把希望当恐惧，
眼看着要胜利，结果还是失败！
我的心犯了多少可怜的错误，
正好当它自以为再幸福不过；
我的眼睛怎样地从眼眶跃出，
当我被疯狂昏乱的热病折磨！
哦，坏事变好事！我现在才知道
善的确常常因恶而变得更善；
被摧毁的爱，一旦重新修建好，
就比原来更宏伟、更美、更强顽。
　　因此，我受了谴责，反心满意足；
　　因祸，我获得过去的三倍幸福。

一二〇

你对我狠过心反而于我有利：
想起你当时使我受到的痛创，
我只好在我的过失下把头低，
既然我的神经不是铜或精钢。
因为，你若受过我狠心的摇撼，
像我所受的，该熬过多苦的日子！
可是我这暴君从没有抽过闲
来衡量你的罪行对我的打击！
哦，但愿我们那悲怛之夜能使我
牢牢记住真悲哀打击得多惨，
我就会立刻递给你，像你递给我，
那抚慰碎了的心的微贱药丹。
　　但你的罪行现在变成了保证，
　　我赎你的罪，你也赎我的败行。

一二一

宁可卑劣，也不愿负卑劣的虚名，
当我们的清白蒙上不白之冤，
当正当的娱乐被人妄加恶声，
不体察我们的感情，只凭偏见。
为什么别人虚伪淫猥的眼睛
有权赞扬或诋毁我活跃的血？
专侦伺我的弱点而比我坏的人
为什么把我认为善的恣意污蔑？
我就是我，他们对于我的诋毁
只能够宣扬他们自己的卑鄙：
我本方正，他们的视线自不轨；
这种坏心眼怎么配把我非议？
　　除非他们固执这糊涂的邪说：
　　恶是人性，统治着世间的是恶。

一二二

你赠我的手册已经一笔一划
永不磨灭地刻在我的心版上，
它将超越无聊的名位的高下，
跨过一切时代，以至无穷无疆：
或者，至少直到大自然的规律
容许心和脑继续存在的一天；
直到它们把你每部分都让给
遗忘，你的记忆将永远不逸散。
可怜的手册就无法那样持久，
我也不用筹码把你的爱登记；
所以你的手册我大胆地放走，
把你交给更能珍藏你的册子：
　　要靠备忘录才不会把你遗忘，
　　岂不等于表明我对你也善忘？

一二三

不，时光，你断不能夸说我在变：
你新建的金字塔，不管多雄壮，
对我一点不稀奇，一点不新鲜；
它们只是旧景象披上了新装。
我们的生命太短促，所以羡慕
你拿来蒙骗我们的那些旧货；
幻想它们是我们心愿的产物，
不肯信从前曾经有人谈起过。
对你和你的纪录我同样不卖账，
过去和现在都不能使我惊奇，
因为你的记载和我所见都扯谎，
都多少是你疾驰中造下的孽迹。
　　我敢这样发誓：我将万古不渝，
　　不管你和你的镰刀多么锋利。

一二四

假如我的爱只是权势的嫡种，
它就会是命运的无父的私生子，
受时光的宠辱所磨折和播弄，
同野草闲花一起任人们采刈。
不呀，它并不是建立在偶然上；
它既不为荣华的笑颜所转移，
也经受得起我们这时代风尚
司空见惯的抑郁、愤懑的打击：
它不害怕那只在短期间有效、
到处散播异端和邪说的权谋，
不因骄阳而生长，雨也冲不掉，
它巍然独立在那里，深思熟筹。
　　被时光愚弄的人们，起来作证！
　　你们毕生作恶，却一死得干净。

一二五

这对我何益，纵使我高擎华盖，
用我的外表来为你妆点门面，
或奠下伟大基础，要留芳万代，
其实比荒凉和毁灭为期更短？
难道我没见过拘守仪表的人，
付出高昂的代价，却丧失一切，
厌弃淡泊而拚命去追求荤辛，
可怜的赢利者，在顾盼[①]中凋谢？
不，请让我在你心里长保忠贞，
收下这份菲薄但由衷的献礼，
它不搀杂次品，也不包藏机心，
而只是你我间互相致送诚意。
　　被收买的告密者，滚开！你越诬告
　　真挚的心，越不能损害它分毫。

① 顾盼　译者为此词作过细心推敲。文汇报版使用“炫耀”，附有作者解释：

原文 in gazing，本应译作“谵望”。但 gaze，根据 Onions，可作 that which is gazed at 解，则 in gazing 或可译作“炫耀”，并似乎与整个形象更凑泊。

译者最后为人文社版选定译文“顾盼”。

一二六[1]

你，小乖乖，时光的无常的沙漏
和时辰（他的小镰刀）都听你左右；
你在亏缺中生长，并昭示大众
你的爱人如何凋零而你向荣；
如果造化（掌握盈亏的大主宰），
在你迈步前进时把你挽回来，
她的目的只是：卖弄她的手法
去丢时光的脸，并把分秒扼杀。
可是你得怕她，你，她的小乖乖！
她只能暂留，并非长保[2]，她的宝贝！
　　她的账目，虽延了期，必须清算：
　　要清偿债务，她就得把你交还。

① 这首诗原缺两行。——译者原注
② 长保　原刊“常保”，据文汇报版修订。

一二七

在远古的时代黑并不算秀俊，
即使算，也没有把美的名挂上；
但如今黑既成为美的继承人，
于是美便招来了侮辱和诽谤。
因为自从每只手都修饰自然，
用艺术的假面貌去美化丑恶，
温馨的美便失掉声价和圣殿，
纵不忍辱偷生，也遭受①了亵渎。
所以我情妇的头发黑如乌鸦，
眼睛也恰好相衬，就像在哀泣
那些生来不美却迷人的冤家，
用假名声去中伤造化的真誉。
　　这哀泣那么配合她们的悲痛，
　　大家齐声说：这就是美的真容。

① 遭受　原刊无“受”字，据文汇报版补正。

一二八

多少次，我的音乐，当你在弹奏
音乐，我眼看那些幸福的琴键
跟着你那轻盈的手指的挑逗，
发出悦耳的旋律，使我魂倒神颠——
我多么艳羡那些琴键轻快地
跳起来狂吻你那温柔的掌心，
而我可怜的嘴唇，本该有这权利，
只能红着脸对琴键的放肆出神！
经不起这引逗，我嘴唇巴不得
做那些舞蹈着的得意小木片，
因为你手指在它们身上轻掠，
使枯木比活嘴唇更值得艳羡。
　　冒失的琴键既由此得到快乐，
　　请把手指给它们，把嘴唇给我。

一二九

把精力消耗在耻辱的沙漠里，
就是色欲在行动；而在行动前，
色欲赌假咒、嗜血、好杀、满身是
罪恶、凶残、粗野、不可靠、走极端；
欢乐尚未央，马上就感觉无味：
毫不讲理地追求；可是一到手，
又毫不讲理地厌恶，像是专为
引上钩者发狂而设下的钓钩；
在追求时疯狂，占有时也疯狂；
不管已有、现有、未有，全不放松；
感受时，幸福；感受完，无上灾殃；
事前，巴望着的欢乐；事后，一场梦。
　　这一切人共知；但谁也不知怎样
　　逃避这个引人下地狱的天堂。

一三〇

我情妇的眼睛一点不像太阳；
珊瑚比她的嘴唇还要红得多：
雪若算白，她的胸就暗褐无光，
发若是铁丝，她头上铁丝婆娑。
我见过红白的玫瑰，轻纱一般；
她颊上却找不到这样的玫瑰；
有许多芳香非常逗引人喜欢，
我情妇的呼吸并没有这香味。
我爱听她谈话，可是我很清楚
音乐的悦耳远胜于她的嗓子；
我承认从没有见过女神走路，
我情妇走路时候却脚踏实地：
　　可是，我敢指天发誓，我的爱侣
　　胜似任何被捧作天仙的美女。

一三一

尽管你不算美，你的暴虐并不
亚于那些因美而骄横的女人；
因为你知道我的心那么糊涂，
把你当作世上的至美和至珍。
不过，说实话，见过你的人都说，
你的脸缺少使爱呻吟的魅力：
尽管我心中发誓反对这说法，
我可还没有公开否认的勇气。
当然我发的誓一点也不欺人；
数不完的呻吟，一想起你的脸，
马上联翩而来，可以为我作证：
对于我，你的黑胜于一切秀妍。
　　你一点也不黑，除了你的人品，
　　可能为了这原故，诽谤才流行。

一三二

我爱上了你的眼睛；你的眼睛
晓得你的心用轻蔑把我磨折，
对我的痛苦表示柔媚的悲悯，
就披上黑色，做旖旎的哭丧者。
而的确，无论天上灿烂的朝阳
多么配合那东方苍白的面容，
或那照耀着黄昏的明星煌煌
（它照破了西方的黯淡的天空），
都不如你的脸配上那双泪眼。
哦，但愿你那颗心也一样为我
挂孝吧，既然丧服能使你增妍，
愿它和全身一样与悲悯配合。
　　黑是美的本质（我那时就赌咒），
　　一切缺少你的颜色的都是丑。

一三三

那使我的心呻吟的心该诅咒，
为了它给我和我朋友[①]的伤痕！
难道光是折磨我一个还不够？
还要把朋友贬为奴隶的身份？
你冷酷的眼睛已夺走我自己，
那另一个我你又无情地霸占：
我已经被他（我自己）和你抛弃；
这使我遭受三三九倍的苦难。
请用你的铁心把我的心包围，
让我可怜的心保释朋友的心；
不管谁监视我，我都把他保卫；
你就不能在狱中再对我发狠。
　　你还会发狠的，我是你的囚徒，
　　我和我的一切必然任你摆布。

① 我朋友　原刊“我的朋友”，据文汇报版修订。

一三四

因此，现在我既承认他属于你，
并照你的意旨把我当抵押品，
我情愿让你把我没收，好教你
释放另一个我来宽慰我的心：
但你不肯放，他又不愿被释放，
因为你贪得无厌，他心肠又软；
他作为保人签字在那证券上，
为了开脱我，反而把自己紧拴。
分毫不放过的高利贷者，你将要
行使你的美丽赐给你的特权
去控诉那为我而负债的知交；
于是我失去他，因为把他欺骗。
　　我把他失掉；你却占有他和我：
　　他还清了债，我依然不得开脱。

一三五

假如女人有满足，你就得如“愿”[1]，
还有额外的心愿，多到数不清；
而多余的我总是要把你纠缠，
想在你心愿的花上添我的锦。
你的心愿汪洋无边，难道不能
容我把我的心愿在里面隐埋？
难道别人的心愿都那么可亲，
而我的心愿就不配你的青睐？
大海，满满是水，照样承受雨点，
好把它的贮藏品大量地增加；
多心愿的你，就该把我的心愿
添上，使你的心愿得到更扩大。
　　别让无情的“不”把求爱者窒息；
　　让众愿同一愿，而我就在这愿里。

① “愿”　此首和下首诗中的“愿”和“心愿”都是原文will字的意译。但will字又是莎士比亚及诗中年轻朋友的名字的简写，因而往往具有双关甚或双关以上的含义。这是当时流行的一种文字游戏。——译者原注

一三六

你的灵魂若骂你我走得太近，
请对你那瞎灵魂说我是你“心愿”，
而“心愿”，她晓得，对她并非陌生；
为了爱，让我的爱如愿吧，心肝。
心愿将充塞你的爱情的宝藏，
请用心愿充满它，把我算一个，
须知道宏大的容器非常便当，
多装或少装一个算不了什么。
请容许我混在队伍中间进去，
不管怎样说我总是其中之一；
把我看作微末不足道，但必须
把这微末看作你心爱的东西。
　　把我名字当你的爱，始终如一，
　　就是爱我，因为“心愿”是我的名字。

一三七

又瞎又蠢的爱，你对我的眸子
干了什么，以致它们视而不见？
它们认得美，也看见美在那里，
却居然错把那极恶当作至善。
我的眼睛若受了偏见的歪扭，
在那人人行驶的海湾里下锚，
你为何把它们的虚妄作成钩，
把我的心的判断力钩得牢牢？
难道是我的心，明知那是公地，
硬把它当作私人游乐的花园？
还是我眼睛否认明显的事实，
硬拿美丽的真蒙住丑恶的脸？
　　我的心和眼既迷失了真方向，
　　自然不得不陷入虚妄的膏肓。

一三八

我爱人赌咒说她浑身是忠实，
我相信她（虽然明知她在撒谎），
让她认为我是个无知的孩子，
不懂得世间种种骗人的勾当。
于是我就妄想她当我还年轻，
虽然明知我盛年已一去不复返；
她的油嘴滑舌我天真地信任：
这样，纯朴的真话双方都隐瞒。
但是为什么她不承认说假话？
为什么我又不承认我已经衰老？
爱的习惯是连信任也成欺诈，
老年谈恋爱最怕把年龄提到。
　　因此，我既欺骗她，她也欺骗我，
　　咱俩的爱情就在欺骗中作乐。

一三九

哦，别叫我原谅你的残酷不仁
对于我的心的不公正的冒犯；
请用舌头伤害我，可别用眼睛；
狠狠打击我，杀我，可别耍手段。
说你已爱上了别人；但当我面，
心肝，可别把眼睛向旁边张望：
何必要耍手段，既然你的强权
已够打垮我过分紧张的抵抗？
让我替你辩解说："我爱人明知
她那明媚的流盼是我的死仇，
才把我的敌人从我脸上转移，
让它向别处放射害人的毒镞！"
　　可别这样；我已经一息奄奄，
　　不如一下盯死我，解除了苦难。

一四〇

你狠心，也该放聪明；别让侮蔑
把我不作声的忍耐逼得太甚；
免得悲哀赐我喉舌，让你领略
我的可怜的痛苦会怎样发狠。
你若学了乖，爱呵，就觉得理应
对我说你爱我，纵使你不如此；
好像暴躁的病人，当死期已近，
只愿听医生报告健康的消息；
因为我若是绝望，我就会发疯，
疯狂中难保不把你胡乱咒骂：
这乖张世界是那么不成体统，
疯狂的耳总爱听疯子的坏话。
　　要我不发疯，而你不遭受诽谤，
　　你得把眼睛正视，尽管心放荡。

一四一

说实话，我的眼睛并不喜欢你，
它们发见你身上百孔和千疮；
但眼睛瞧不起的，心儿却着迷，
它一味溺爱，不管眼睛怎样想。
我耳朵也不觉得你嗓音好听，
就是我那容易受刺激的触觉，
或味觉，或嗅觉都不见得高兴
参加你身上任何官能的盛酌。
可是无论我五种机智或五官
都不能劝阻痴心去把你侍奉，
我昂藏的丈夫仪表它再不管，
只甘愿作你傲慢的心的仆从。
　　不过我的灾难也非全无好处：
　　她引诱我犯罪，也教会我受苦。

一四二

我的罪咎是爱，你的美德是憎，
你憎我的罪，为了我多咎的爱：
哦，你只要比一比你我的实情，
就会发觉责备我多么不应该。
就算应该，也不能出自你嘴唇，
因为它们亵渎过自己的口红，
劫夺过别人床笫应得的租金，
和我一样屡次偷订爱的假盟。
我爱你，你爱他们，都一样正当，
尽管你追求他们而我讨你厌。
让哀怜的种子在你心里暗长，
终有天你的哀怜也得人哀怜。
　　假如你只知追求，自己却吝啬，
　　你自己的榜样就会招来拒绝。

一四三

看呀，像一个小心翼翼的主妇
跑着去追撵一只逃走的母鸡，
把孩子扔下，拚命快跑，要抓住
那个她急着要得回来的东西；
被扔下的孩子紧跟在她后头，
哭哭啼啼要赶上她，而她只管
望前一直追撵，一步也不停留，
不顾她那可怜的小孩的不满：
同样，你追那个逃避你的家伙，
而我（你的孩子）却在后头追你；
你若赶上了希望，请回头照顾我，
尽妈妈的本分，轻轻吻我，很和气。
　　只要你回头来抚慰我的悲啼，
　　我就会祷告神让你从心所欲。

一四四

两个爱人像精灵般把我诱惑，
一个叫安慰，另外一个叫绝望：
善的天使是个男子，丰姿绰约；
恶的幽灵是个女人，其貌不扬。
为了促使我早进地狱，那女鬼
引诱我的善精灵硬把我抛开，
还要把他迷惑，使沦落为妖魅，
用肮脏的骄傲追求纯洁的爱。
我的天使是否已变成了恶魔，
我无法一下子确定，只能猜疑；
但两个都把我扔下，互相结合，
一个想必进了另一个的地狱。
　　可是这一点我永远无法猜透，
　　除非是恶的天使把善的撵走。

一四五

爱神亲手捏就的嘴唇
对着为她而憔悴的我，
吐出了这声音说，“我恨”：
但是她一看见我难过，
心里就马上大发慈悲，
责备那一向都是用来
宣布甜蜜的判词的嘴，
教它要把口气改过来：
“我恨”，她又把尾巴补缀，
那简直像明朗的白天
赶走了魔鬼似的黑夜，
把它从天堂甩进阴间。
　　她把“我恨”的恨字摒弃，
　　救了我的命说，“不是你”。

一四六

可怜的灵魂，万恶身躯的中心，
被围攻你的叛逆势力所俘掳，
为何在暗中憔悴，忍受着饥馑，
却把外壁妆得那么堂皇丽都？
赁期那么短，这倾颓中的大厦
难道还值得你这样铺张浪费？
是否要让蛆虫来继承这奢华，
把它吃光？这可是肉体的依皈？
所以，灵魂，请拿你仆人来度日，
让他消瘦，以便充实你的贮藏，
拿无用时间来兑换永久租期，
让内心得滋养，别管外表堂皇：
　　这样，你将吃掉那吃人的死神，
　　而死神一死，世上就永无死人。

一四七

我的爱是一种热病，它老切盼
那能够使它长期保养的单方，
服食一种能维持病状的药散，
使多变的病态食欲长久盛旺。
理性（那医治我的爱情的医生）
生气我不遵守他给我的嘱咐，
把我扔下，使我绝望，因为不信
医药的欲望，我知道，是条死路。
我再无生望，既然丧失了理智，
整天都惶惑不安、烦躁、疯狂；
无论思想或谈话，全像个疯子，
脱离了真实，无目的，杂乱无章；
　　因为我曾赌咒说你美，说你璀璨，
　　你却是地狱一般黑，夜一般暗。

一四八

唉，爱把什么眼睛装在我脑里，
使我完全认不清真正的景象？
说认得清吧，理智又窜往哪里，
竟错判了眼睛所见到的真相？
如果我眼睛所迷恋的真是美，
为何大家都异口同声不承认？
若真不美呢，那就绝对无可讳，
爱情的眼睛不如一般人看得真：
当然喽，它怎能够，爱眼怎能够
看得真呢，它日夜都泪水汪汪？
那么，我看不准又怎算得稀有？
太阳也要等天晴才照得明亮。
　　狡猾的爱神！你用泪把我弄瞎，
　　只因怕明眼把你的丑恶揭发。

一四九

你怎能，哦，狠心的，否认我爱你，
当我和你协力把我自己厌恶？
我不是在想念你，当我为了你
完全忘掉我自己，哦，我的暴主？
我可曾把那恨你的人当朋友？
我可曾对你厌恶的人献殷勤？
不仅这样，你对我一皱起眉头，
我不是马上叹气，把自己痛恨？
我还有什么可以自豪的优点，
傲慢到不屑于为你服役奔命，
既然我的美都崇拜你的缺陷，
唯你的眼波的流徒转移是听？
　　但，爱呵，尽管憎吧，我已猜透你：
　　你爱那些明眼的，而我是瞎子。

一五〇

哦，从什么威力你取得这力量，
连缺陷也能把我的心灵支配？
教我诬蔑我可靠的目光撒谎，
并矢口否认太阳使白天明媚？
何来这化臭腐为神奇的本领，
使你的种种丑恶不堪的表现
都具有一种灵活强劲的保证，
使它们，对于我，超越一切至善？
谁教你有办法使我更加爱你，
当我听到和见到你种种可憎？
哦，尽管我钟爱着人家所嫌弃，
你总不该嫌弃我，同人家一条心：
　　既然你越不可爱，越使得我爱，
　　你就该觉得我更值得你喜爱。

一五一

爱神太年轻，不懂得良心是什么；
但谁不晓得良心是爱情所产？
那么，好骗子，就别专找我的错，
免得我的罪把温婉的你也牵连。
因为，你出卖了我，我的笨肉体
又哄我出卖我更高贵的部分；
我灵魂叮嘱我肉体，说它可以
在爱情上胜利；肉体再不作声，
一听见你的名字就马上指出
你是它的胜利品；它趾高气扬，
死心蹋地作你最鄙贱的家奴，
任你颐指气使，或倒在你身旁。
　　所以我可问心无愧地称呼她
　　作“爱”，我为她的爱起来又倒下。

一五二

你知道我对你的爱并不可靠，
但你赌咒爱我，这话更靠不住；
你撕掉床头盟，又把新约毁掉，
既结了新欢，又种下新的憎恶。
但我为什么责备你两番背盟，
自己却背了二十次！最反复是我；
我对你一切盟誓都只是滥用，
因而对于你已经失尽了信约。
我曾矢口作证你对我的深爱：
说你多热烈、多忠诚、永不变卦，
我使眼睛失明，好让你显光彩，
教眼睛发誓，把眼前景说成虚假——
　　我发誓说你美！还有比这荒唐：
　　抹煞真理去坚持那么黑的谎！

一五三

爱神放下他的火炬，沉沉睡去：
月神的一个仙女乘了这机会
赶快把那枝煽动爱火的火炬
浸入山间一道冷冰冰的泉水；
泉水，既从这神圣的火炬得来
一股不灭的热，就永远在燃烧，
变成了沸腾的泉，一直到现在
还证实具有起死回生的功效。
但这火炬又在我情妇眼里点火，
为了试验，爱神碰一下我胸口，
我马上不舒服，又急躁又难过，
一刻不停地跑向温泉去求救，
　　但全不见效：能治好我的温泉
　　只有新燃起爱火的我情人的眼。

一五四

小小爱神有一次呼呼地睡着，
把点燃心焰的火炬放在一边，
一群蹁跹的贞洁的仙女恰巧
走过；其中最美丽[①]的一个天仙
用她处女的手把那曾经烧红
万千颗赤心的火炬偷偷拿走，
于是这玩火小法师在酣睡中
便缴械给那贞女的纤纤素手。
她把火炬往附近冷泉里一浸，
泉水被爱神的烈火烧得沸腾，
变成了温泉，能消除人间百病；
但我呵，被我情妇播弄得头疼，
　　跑去温泉就医，才把这点弄清：
　　爱烧热泉水，泉水冷不了爱情。

① 最美丽　原刊无“丽”字，据文汇报版补正。